QUANTUM ROOTS II

I0621695

KYLE   KEYES

QUANTUM ROOTS II

kylekeyes.com

KYLE   KEYES

QUANTUM ROOTS II

PRELUDE

Monkey see, monkey do.

Headline grabbers are often followed by copy cat artists, seeking attention in a world too busy to notice anything but crime.

Olan Chapman put Hobbs Creek on the national map when the slender computer programmer reverted back to a former identity as Jesse Joe Jacks. Chapman used this alter-ego to avenge the rape/murder of his childhood sister. Chapman then went over Niagara Falls in a small outboard and a rain of bullets. After which, copy cat vigilantes sprang up in dark alleys from sea to shining sea.

Noted psychologists of the day believed that Olan Chapman was a sign of the times. The message was clear. The commonwealth had lost faith in the system, and public sentiment was now ready for a vigilante.

KYLE KEYES

The sightings all but faded into obscurity at one point. Then, fresh fingerprints reached the FIC office of Paranormal Director, Alexis Grumman,

The fingerprints belonged to Olan Chapman.

In this sequel to *Quantum Roots*, noted physicist, Norman Arnold Daly convinces the Federal Intelligence Commission that there is no universe. Simply put by Daly, we live in an energy field that produces star systems from recycled quarks. Planets, water and living species follow in sequence as hadrons squeeze through two dimensional wormholes.

Director Grumman is somewhat skeptical at first, but eventually concludes that computer programmer, Olan Chapman has multiple personalities, when he shows up as U.S. Marshall, Samuel Leroy McCoy.

QUANTUM ROOTS II

KYLE   KEYES

QUANTUM ROOTS II

Dedicated To Frances

KYLE   KEYES

CHAPTER 1

Female footsteps echoed off dark alley walls.

Three boys waited behind a shadowy dumpster,

Lights flickered out and steel gates closed, as stores locked up shop for the day. The alley led from a city artery to a back street, parking lot. Not many locals used this shortcut for fear of being raped, robbed or killed. Lighting was sparse and ground windows were boarded over.

High heels reached the dumpster.

The boys sprang.

KYLE KEYES

The woman screamed, her packages falling to the concrete paving. One boy covered the woman's mouth. A second boy grabbed her handbag. The third boy yanked off her bra.

"Damn Chico," cried the third boy, "Look at these tits!"

One boy sounded the wolf howl and two more boys came from no-where. Cried Chico, "What took you so long?"

"We ran into a nosy tramp at the end of the alley," said a boy with a nose ring, "I dropped him with a rabbit punch to the gut. Then we stomped on him for being on our turf !"

The five boys wrestled the woman downward to a prone position. Grappling hands pinned her arms and legs onto the cold concrete. The Latino called Chico pulled off the woman's panties. Her bare cheeks sparkled as a passing headlamp shed light down the alley. Her screams again filled the night air as hungry fingers moved from her mouth to her breasts.

"Chico, let me go first," said an Oriental with pubic hair but no whiskers. He stood over the woman, his trousers down, penis in hand. He wore pink under-wear and a belly tattoo that read *MOM*. "I am Wolfpack leader and I should go first."

QUANTUM ROOTS II

"Chico goes first," panted Chico as a window light flickered two stories up, "I have the lead role, so I go first."

"Chico," whispered a black youth looking sky-ward, "Someone is watching from that balcony."

"That will be Romano," said Chico placing a knife blade against the woman's throat, "He will shoot the film. You Wolf Pack members will soon be head-liners back in Havana. Your names will get top billing right next to my name."

"My family will be proud," crowed an Indian boy simply named Apache, "Our ancestors plundered many a wagon train in many a movie, and my great, great, great grandfather scalped many a pony express rider."

"Can we cut the chatter down there," came a voice from overhead.

"But what an honor," continued the Indian boy, "Never did I dream of working with Chico Gondolas Mendez, world renowned porn star."

"I said to cut the chatter down there !"

One story up, a shadowy figure named Romano hastened to setup a tripod, camera and spotlights. One tripod leg collapsed and the porno film maker used his trouser belt to strap the metal rig to the porch railing.

He then yelled down, "We need all clothes off, victim and attackers."

"Romano, it 'es cold down here."

"Our client wants bare skin shots," insisted the porno film maker, "I will be using two spotlights. One on the woman, and one on the penis as it moves in from the shadows. If you can't get an erection, you don't get paid. . .and Chico, where are your black lace panties?"

"Romano, I am not a fairy !"

"You were told to wear the black lace panties," yelled down the projectionist, "We are under contract here, Chico. We give our client what he wants or we do not get paid."

Romano's buyer was a man named John Smith from Silicone Valley, California. Smith wanted the movie shot somewhere on the opposite coast by a black market film maker from out of the country. Romano got the job via an anonymous porn star who once worked under the infamous, Chico Gondolas Mendez, known throughout Cuba as the Porno King. Film details were then worked out by cousin Romano, including little blue capsules that would arouse sexual desire.

"I don't think my pill is working," said a Latino holding his crotch.

QUANTUM ROOTS II

"Phew!" cried the boy wearing the nose ring, "What is that odor?"

"I think she needs a bath," said another gang member.

"We're rolling !" yelled Romano, "And again I remind you, if you can't get it up, you don't get paid."

Arms and legs thrashed about in the darkness. The woman bit into a finger and a howl turned into a chain of profanities. Backhand slaps followed, as many hands locked down wrists and ankles. Soon, the woman lay tied and naked, legs open. The first spot light came on. The bright cone illuminated the woman's face. Suddenly, Chico jumped up bellowing, "This es not our cousin Rosemary !"

Romano Gondolas Mendez stopped filming. He pushed a red beanie cap off bushy eyebrows and hit the pause button on the high-tech camera. His heavy rim glasses all but slid off his skinny nose as he peered over the balcony railing to cry down, "This 'es not our cousin Rosemary?"

"This es not Rosemary,"

"Who es it ?" asked Romano.

Chico took his hand off the woman's mouth to ask, "Who are you?"

The woman screamed.

Chico covered her mouth.

"Damn," cried Romano, "I thought you had all your chicks in a row, Chico."

"I think you mean ducks,"

"Whatever."

"So, what now?" asked Chico.

Romano surveyed the scene below. The strange woman lay naked, surrounded by a ring of eager young males. Pants were down, penises up. Romano hit the movie button and said, "Put a gag on her and do her. Our buyer is anxious to get this film."

"I think that's rape," cautioned Chico.

"So, rape her !" said Romano.

"Owww!" cried Chico, "She just kneed me."

The Latino with the nose ring was first to notice the shadow approaching. The silhouette was that of a holster strapped low to a man's trouser leg. Yelled the Latino, "We have an intruder, Chico!"

"Let the lady up," ordered the shadow.

"What 'es this ?" panted Chico mounting the naked woman to begin the assault, "Who said that?"

"Who said that?" asked Wolf Pack members as one voice.

"Who said that?" queried Romano from the balcony over head.

QUANTUM ROOTS II

A slim figure stood a short distance down the alley. Feet spread. Left hand near a Colt 45 that was fast becoming a Buffalo City legend. A black stetson shaded his stubble face. Both his voice and eyes held steady as he said, "Now help the lady up."

"Help the lady up?" cried Chico, "Theese es not in the script,"

"Will someone get this hobo off the set," called down Romano, "Then get set up so we can shoot this scene again."

Chico jumped to his feet, cursing. His jock strap ankle-cuffed one hairy leg, which sent the Cuban porn actor into a hopping mode to keep from falling. The other gang members began to giggle which only added to Chico's anger.

"Okay Wyatt Earp," sputtered Chico catching balance by placing one foot on the woman's stomach, "Take your gun and your badge and get your boy scout ass out of here."

"Last chance," said the vigilante "Let the lady up."

"Theese is not a lady," lied Chico, "Theese is my third cousin from Havana. Her name is Rosemary Gondolas Mendez. My name is Chico Mendez. We're all family, here. Now scram."

KYLE KEYES

"Time's up," said the vigilante, "Fill your hand."

"Fill my hand ?!!!

There's always a point where the road gives way to the rage. Chico swooped up the discarded knife from the alley floor. The knife was not real. However, the hard rubber prop was balanced for throwing, and Chico Gondolas Mendez was known throughout Cuba for his knife throwing expertise – along with his giant penis. One story has it that Chico once split a hock from a first knife throw, with the blade from a second knife throw. *Believe it or not*. He stood now with feet spread for balance, and hurled the knife at the vigilante.

All held a collective breath.

Suddenly, a Colt 45 jumped into the vigilante's hand. The first shot took out the rubber missile in mid air. The second shot hit the porn star right between the eyes.

Silence.

Blood shot onto the grimy pavement.

Chico crumbled like glass turning to sand.

Multiple screams broke the silence.

"Oh my god !" screamed Romano as shots three, four and five dropped the Latino, the Oriental and the black youth. A fast reload took out the final two gang members who were on the dead run toward Main

Street. Continued Romano waving arms and screaming, "We are making a movie. This is just a film flick for the porn market !"

The vigilante looked up as more window lights came on - lights that illuminated Romano's tripod and two floodlight stands. The vigilante holstered the Colt 45 . He spun on a boot heel and disappeared.

Quickly, Romano packed up gear as new screams sounded from below. He peered over the iron railing to see cousin Rosemary kneeing over cousin Chico. Yelled Romano, "What the hell happened ?"

"He killed Chico !" screamed Rosemary.

"I know he killed Chico," shouted Romano, "I thought he was going to kill me !"

"I didn't want to come to this country," sobbed Rosemary, "I wanted to do this film in Havana. This was your idea to come across the border."

"Our buyer wanted it shot here," said Romano, "Where have you been ! . . and where did this white woman come from ?"

"He killed Chico," moaned Rosemary sitting in a puddle of blood next to her cousin.

"Rosemary! Where did this white woman come from? "

Sirens sounded in the distance.

KYLE KEYES

"We need to split," said Romano talking over muffled screams coming from the rape victim.

"I'm staying with Chico," sobbed Rosemary.

"Suit yourself," cried Romano, "I'm going."

Soon, the alley filled with flashing blue lights, EMS squads, a fire truck, news reporters and nosy onlookers who monitor police calls. First responders checked out the naked woman, then loaded her onto a stretcher. Local police officers took Cousin Rosemary Mendez into custody, as she shielded her face from social media and film hawks.

Cousin Romano Mendez vanished, along with the film.

Chapter 2

Federal Intelligence Center: Warrenton, Virginia

Jeremy Wade gunned his motor scooter up the concrete steps of FIC Headquarters. He paused at the first landing to salute a warrant officer and pinch a slow walking secretary in the posterior. When he reached the top, he leaned the noisy scooter against a giant planter, and removed a bicycle helmet. He smacked down a springy hair cowlick, and headed toward the revolving door.

"Whoa," said the entrance guard.

"Whoa?" laughed Jeremy flashing ID, "Stanley, I think you mean *halt who goes there*."

"That was a nice piece of driving," said the door guard, "Now you can drive that scooter back down to the parking lot."

"I have a permit to park here," said Jeremy.

"Your handle bars are crushing the plants," said the door guard.

"Stanley, there are no plants in the planter," said the special agent.

"Well, there could be."

"Stanley, the general doesn't want this baby left in the parking lot."

"Show me the permit," said the guard.

Jeremy brushed aside a red tie and checked an inside suit pocket. He slapped trouser pockets and opened a wallet, over stocked with credit cards. He found the permit in a rear pocket, and handed the rumpled paper to the guard.

"You must be sleeping with the right people," said the door guard looking over the permit, "When are you gonna get a muffler for that scooter ?"

"This is not a scooter."

"Looks like a scooter."

"Stanley, this is a special government issue – high tech- state of the art – hot pursuit, vehicle," explained the junior agent proudly, "This baby has front end fire power, tear gas missiles, and a turbo boost engine that tops out just under 200 mph. And, it can actually fly short distances, given the open air space."

"Looks like a scooter," said the guard, "What's in the saddle bags?"

"Classified," replied Jeremy.

"Of course," said the guard.

Sudden truck horns shattered the quiet morning air, followed by a loud crash coming from the nearby Eastern Bypass. Screams came next, then distant sirens as busy dispatchers responded to panic buttons. The security guard lowered ear flaps on his snow cap and muttered, "Don't know why they built this place right off the freeway and this permit doesn't say you can park here."

"Stanley, General Grumman issued the permit."

"Who?"

"Alexis," said Jeremy in louder tones, "Alexis Grumman, Lt General,"

"I can read that," said the door guard, "But it doesn't say you can park here. It says you can park in the lobby."

"Stanley, I can't do that."

"Why not ?"

"I can't get through the door."

"No need to get sore,?" said the guard, "I'm just doing my job."

"I didn't say sore," cried Jeremy, "I said door and will you take off the ear muffs! Security guards do not wear ear muffs. You look like the Red Baron."

KYLE   KEYES

"Lobby or the parking lot," said the door guard taking off his ear covers,   "You are not parking that eye sore out here."

Sighing, Jeremy and his motor scooter squeezed into the first compartment of the revolving door. A fat man with stocky arms was just leaving. The unknown intruder had slipped by Stanley, only to be turned back at a second checkpoint, which led to a main hall that led to department checkpoints. The stocky intruder was now back in the revolving door, rejected and angry. He grabbed the hand bar and shoved. The door spun full circle. The fat man made a clean exit and stormed by Stanley.   Jeremy finished the wild ride on the floor, pinned down by the scooter.

"Hey, this is a checkpoint,"   yelled Stanley at the fat man descending the steps.

Yelled Jeremy at Stanley, "Stop worrying about that guy and get Rocko over here, and tell him to bring a crow bar. The scooter's jammed in the door track. My leg's jammed under the scooter, and I need to get to the assembly room."

"I'm sure your girlfriend will wait," said Stanley.

"Alexis and I are not girlfriend and boyfriend." lied Jeremy,   "FIC policy prohibits intimacy between agents assigned to mutual departments."

QUANTUM ROOTS II

"You share the same laundromat," said Stanley.

"How do you know that?"

"I get around and for what it's worth, Rocko went home early," said the door guard, "He has a tooth issue."

"A tooth issue?" whined Jeremy, "Rocko only has one tooth."

"Yes, and that one tooth is bothering him."

"Well, get somebody from maintenance over here," cried Jeremy," I need to get to that meeting."

"Time's up," said a female voice coming from Jeremy Wade's classified communicator, "I'm starting the meeting without you."

*   *   *   *   *

The Department For Paranormal Activities now sits on the third floor of the F.I.C. building, due to second floor expansion of satellite imagery. The DPA offices are loaded with scanners, computers and wall screens that connect to a virtual networking system. Lt General Alexis Grumman heads up this small agency which interfaces with FBI, CIA and numerous other branches of the nation's Intelligence Community. (IC).

KYLE KEYES

She stood now addressing an array of noisy agents borrowed from other federal agencies. As days go, this day was going south fast, like a smiley face turning upside down: the heating element burned out in her one-cup coffee maker; she had on the bra with the bad snap; her key assistant, Jeremy Wade was stuck in the revolving door downstairs, and she couldn't be sure if he locked up upon leaving her apartment. She swirled some ice fragments in a glass tumbler, took a sip, popped a candy mint between her pale lips and said, "I think introductions are in order. .so. . I'll start it off."

No response.

She spoke again.

Chatter continued.

She left the room and walked along the balcony railing that circles the third floor, sub stations for other federal agencies. Down below, a flurry of white and blue shirts monitored world events on numerous wall screens via satellite. Sounds of bullets and battle filtered upward. She moved on. One third floor office remained unfinished. She grabbed a short length of 2 by 4, and returned to the noisy DPA conference room. Deftly, she swung the wooden stud onto a desk top, with a resounding crash.

QUANTUM ROOTS II

All fell silent.

"I think introductions are in order," she said popping a second candy mint while sipping ice water, "I'll start it off."

Alexis Grumman was among the first United States women to earn the rank of Lieutenant General in the armed forces. The three star, single mother served tours in Korea, Germany and Vietnam. She wore the Legion Of Merit, and two Meritorious Service medals on her smart uniform jacket. She served much of her military career coordinating intelligence with remote field operations. She finished by saying, "So here I am having meaningful talks about UFO sightings and river monster uprisings."

Laughter erupted.

"Who's next ?" asked Alexis.

A thin man with receding hair and eager eyes jumped to his feet. Said the federal agent, "Spicer CIA. Just got back from North Africa. Previously, I worked with Colonel Swan on *Operation Black Ice.*"

The lady general's eyebrows raised. She asked if anybody else had worked with Colonel Martin Swan. Several hands shot up. Said Alexis, "Rise and state your names and specialties."

"Kingsley," said the first man, "Explosives."

KYLE KEYES

"Swiggert," said the second man, "Sniper."

Alexis Grumman frowned. She and Martin Swan both worked out of an FIC manual that spelled out the department's conduct and procedure rules. However, Lt General Grumman and Colonel Martin Swan stood pages apart. While Alexis adhered to the letter of the law, Swan's *Invisible Six* Unit was dis-banned in early 2009 for conduct violations unbecoming to federal agents. Eventually, Swan's unit was reinstated after General James "Iron Horse" Taylor agreed to revise the manual with help from several congressional, hearing members, to overlook agents working undercover.

"I also worked with the Invisible Six team," said agent Reuben Goldberg coming back from the water cooler, "We were on the recent *White House Patrol* mission. Such an honor it was to be working with the infamous Martin Swan."

"Yes, we have film of you urinating behind the bushes," said Alexis.

"I have a bladder infection."

"Are you waiting for desk duty?' asked Alexis.

"No ma'am," replied the pudgy agent, "I'm here for more field experience before I begin my Navy Seal training."

QUANTUM ROOTS II

Alexis Grumman stared at Reuben Goldberg The junior agent had a triple chin and a posterior too wide to fit the black leather chairs, which were stock items for the conference room. Thus, Reuben sat on a stool with no arm rests and little foot support. His heavy feet dangled inches from the floor. Sweat rings circled his arm pits. Said the lady general, "You realize a navy seal undergoes rigorous training for that qualification. It's not all cake and icing. You must graduate from a twenty four week, underwater demolition school, a basic parachuting course, and twenty six weeks of seal qualification training."

"I do have one issue," admitted Goldberg.

"I thought you might."

"I don't like water up my nose."

Alexis rolled her brown eyes toward a ceiling fan, sighed, sipped more ice water and quietly said, "Report to the gym in the morning."

"Yes, ma'am."

"Who's next?"

"Agent Richard Kramer."

"And what do you do, agent?"

"Pilot."

"Pilot," mused Alexis Grumman, "If memory serves correct, you fly for Colonel Martin Swan and the

KYLE KEYES

Invisible Six.

"Yes ma'am," said a man with hair longer than a teenager with a cause, "I flew the *mid-flight abductee recovery mission.*"

"We seem to have a number of Colonel Swan's men here," said Alexis, "Just for credentials sake, can you give me a run down on that mission, Kramer?"

The story goes that four terrorists kidnapped an ambassador's daughter in Frankfurt, Germany. They then commandeered an Ariana airliner and headed for Afghanistan. Sometime later, when radio contact was re-established, the plane landed safely in Kabul International Airport. The girl was back at the American embassy in Germany. The four terrorist were dead in the baggage compartment.

"And just how was that done?" asked Alexis.

"That's classified information," said Kramer.

"Agent, everybody in this room has a security clearance," reminded the lady general, "Or at least they better."

"Of course," said the pilot.

The *mid-flight abductee recovery mission* stands out as the *Invisible Six's* most magical escapade. But, like all magic, the bottom line was illusion. Pack leader, Martin Swan used advance information to conceal two operators on the stolen Ariana air jet. Swan's agents retook the plane and locked the four terrorists in the baggage compartment. They first landed the plane in a remote airstrip, where the girl was transferred to a second jet and returned to Germany. Concluded Kramer

"I then flew the Ariana aircraft on to Kabul. Where we completed the mission."

"The original report denied a midway landing," said Alexis.

"We lied about that," replied the ace pilot.

"And just how did the four terrorists die?"

"They suffocated inside their black hoods."

"Bravo," said Alexis, "Who's next ?"

One by one, each agent presented their name, department and qualifications. When the last agent sat down, Alexis spoke for her assistant, Jeremy Wade who wasn't present. Jeremy was a high school valedictorian, dominated the dean's list in college, and earned his master's degree at MIT before before becoming a federal agent. His shortfalls were gun handling and vehicle control. However, Alexis was quick to point out that Agent Wade was a valuable cog in the *Federal Intelligence Commission* machine.

"Sounds like a brain," suggested agent Reuben Goldberg.

"Probably a Mensa," verified Alexis, "Anyway, agent Wade will join us shortly. . .as soon as he gets his motor scooter out of the revolving door."

"We're ready to roll," cried a nearby voice.

"We need to cover a few issues before we hit the screening room," said Alexis, "By now you all know why we are here. Namely, this renewed outbreak of vigilante shootings which started a week ago in Buffalo, N.Y. The shootings then crossed state lines and have now captioned national headlines."

"Ma'am, I understand jurisdiction stipulations," said CIA Agent Spicer, "But why does this come under the department for paranormal activities?"

"You have been overseas?"

"Yes ma'am."

"Current shootings match those of a vigilante who died two years back,," explained Alexis Grumman, "Same MO, same weapon caliber, same dress attire. And, we have some film clips. "

"That's paranormal," whistled Spicer.

"Which brings us to the next issue," said the lady general staring at agents Kingsley and Swiggert, "This vigilante is a person of interest. We don't want him shot, and we don't want him blown up."

"Yes ma'am,"

"Yes ma'am."

"Happy to have you aboard," said Alexis, "Now let's get down to the real nitty gritty. We don't have much on that first shooting, which took place in an east Buffalo City alley. The photographer ran off with the film. We do have the eye-witness testimony of a Cuban female actress, named Rosemary Gondolas Mendez. Supposedly, she and seven associates wanted to film a porno flick aimed at the black market. She would be the victim. Her cousin Chico had the lead role which called for a rapist with a dead conscience and a lively penis. Her cousin Romano would film the assault, which also included five local gang members who called them-selves the Wolf Pack."

"Question," came a voice from the rear.

"Yes, Agent Spicer."

"This Rosemary was going to have sex with all six boys."

"One man and five boys," clarified Alexis.

"Isn't that a bit much?"

"Agent Spicer, there is a Polish porn star who had sex with 919 men in under 12 hours," said Alexis smiling, "And, she's happily married from what I under stand."

"You're shitting me."

"Google it," said Alexis, "And curb your tongue, soldier."

"Damn, now I'm wondering where my wife is on *ladies night out*," said Agent Spicer.

Again, laughter erupted.

Alexis paused for more ice water and another candy mint. She put the subject matter back on track with a bizarre statement from Rosemary Gondolas Mendez, taken under oath. The Cuban porn star claimed to be menstruating when it came time to shoot the movie. Somehow, she struck up a fast acquaintance with a white woman headed for the same dark, parking lot. Rosemary convinced the woman to cut through the back alley to save time. Once in the alley, Rosemary hung back, which left the white woman to go on ahead, alone.

"So, Rosemary saw the whole assault?" asked Agent Swiggert.

"She did."

"I'm surprised she stuck around," said Kingsley on loan from the FBI.

"She wanted to watch cousin Chico *do a white woman*," said Alexis, "And that's a quote-unquote."

"This Rosemary is not a very nice person," said Agent Goldberg breaking the sudden silence.

QUANTUM ROOTS II

"Reuben, these are porn people," explained the lady general, "They live in a XX*X* world, with their own code of ethics."

"How many boys had sexual intercourse with the woman?" asked Spicer on loan from the CIA.

"They all did according to Rosemary Mendez's statement," said Alexis Grumman tapping a fax sheet, "She claims that she watched each boy rape the woman, while the others held her arms and legs. However, this does not align with Buffalo hospital records, which show no sperm samples taken from the victim."

"Why would she lie?" asked Agent Kingsley.

"According to Ms Mendez," said Alexis "Cousin Romano wanted the movie to start and end with the lead actor. Oddly enough, she falsified her statement to follow the script. We don't know why. We do know that the vigilante showed up. Threats exchanged. Chico threw a prop knife at the intruder, who shot from the waist and dropped all six boys in mere seconds."

"Without reloading?" asked agent Hendricks from the F.B.I., "It's customary to keep one chamber empty in a six shooter."

"Ms Mendez does not remember a reload," said Alexis, "However, the vigilante fired a total of seven bullets, which means he must have reloaded his gun at some point in time."

"Maybe, this Mendez woman ran when the fireworks started," suggested Agent Hendricks, "Which means her eye witness account is tainted."

"Maybe," conceded Alexis, "But we all know what trauma does to recall, and Ms Mendez no doubt lost it when fantasy turned to fact."

"This shooting sounds like the *point and shoot* technique," said agent Carlson from the west coast, "We have cowboy clubs back home who specialize in the quick draw. I can't get the hang of it, but those who can, can. I've seen a man fire from the waist, and shoot a dime out of the air."

"Sounds to me like a good lawsuit," said Agent Spicer, "Lawyers from here to Cuba will make out on this one."

"Maybe," said Alexis, "Maybe not. The Mendez family was up from Florida with no papers. They were visiting another illegal immigrant in the Buffalo area. Now, the whole group faces deportation back to Cuba, unless our country chooses to prosecute rather than deport, which could be red tape tied to red tape."

"I need the bathroom," requested Goldberg.

"We'll be in the screen room when you get back," said Alexis, "The rest rooms have a key code."

"Yes ma'am."

"Do you know the code?"

"No ma'am."

"Marcie our desk clerk will give it to you "

"Yes ma'am."

The screen room sat just behind the conference room and linked to the worldwide systems board, one level down. Chairs formed a velvet arc that resembled your local movie theater. Doug, the invisible computer projectionist could bring up almost any scenario requested, today or yesteryear. Pictures of a restaurant massacre played across the screen as Reuben Goldberg returned.

"I wish this vigilante would have showed up a bit sooner," said Reuben Goldberg sitting down, "He could have saved the day."

"The cavalry's not always on time," replied the lady general, "This is not the movies, Reuben. And now moving on. . . Doug, run the security film from the New Hampshire shooting."

"It's not in HD," called out the male voice from behind the scenes, "But here it is. Ignore the fog and the water spots on the camera lens."

Six boys drove up to the family amusement park in a bouncy ATV, with a roll bar for a roof and no muffler. They screeched to a stop before a freshly painted sign that read: FAMILY FUN LAND. A second sign read *Closed For The Season*. An old man worked on an idle roller coaster. Empty kiosks lined each side of the main walkway. A Ferris wheel hovered over a steel drum filled with rain water. Phone pole posters advertised two new rides: Skyfall and the Amazon Water Ride Adventure.

There was no security guard in sight.

The six boys bailed out of the ATV and hurdled a low spot in the raggedy cyclone fence. They were a noisy collection of fresh tattoos, nose rings and dirty sneakers. They wore an arm patch that read Wild Bunch. It was Saturday afternoon. The boys were restless and bored and *on* something.

Pantomime often tells the story. The boys were there to try out the new rides.

The old man wiped off greasy hands while sizing up the intruders. Verbal confrontation followed. The old man pointed to an exit gate, while reaching for his cell phone. The boys grabbed the old man and headed for the rain barrel.

"They dragged him by the arms," said Alexis, filling in for some film failure, "You can see the tiny ruts his shoe heels carved into the sand."

QUANTUM ROOTS II

The six boys dropped the old man head first into the rainwater barrel. Laughing, they held his thrashing feet until air bubbles ceased to surface. Then they ran for the rides.

"His name was Frank Kavenaugh," said Alexis referring to the maintenance man, "He leaves behind a wife, two kids and four grandchildren. He was two months from retirement."

"I need the bathroom again," begged Goldberg with one hand on his crotch, "I think it was the water barrel. The sound of water makes me go. Sometimes, I go three or four times when it rains. And fountains are a real no-no. I can't even hangout with the water cooler gang, or stand near a lawn sprinkler."

"Thank you for sharing that with us, agent."

"Yes Ma'am,"

"And Agent Goldberg?"

"Yes Ma'am?"

"Permission granted to leave the room," replied Alexis, then to the camera man, "Doug, fast forward to the vigilante's appearance."

"Roger."

The surveillance cameras failed to pick up the vigilante gunning down the first boy. The film showed the body falling from above, and hitting the dirt with a thud. Seconds later, a flat brim hat and Colt 45 came into view facing the merry-go-round. The six boys had tired of Skyfall and split into pairs. Two hopped aboard a roller coaster. Two climbed onto the merry-go-round. One boy rode the Ferris wheel, while the other boy worked the controls.

"The bodies at the Ferris wheel were identified as the Boxby brothers," said Alexis, "They are reported to be homosexual, which explains the large earrings in the right ear. Also strange, the vigilante shot one out of the bucket, and saved the one who worked the controls for last. We can only guess that his screams failed to alert the others."

Authorities found two bodies hanging from pony stirrups on the merry-go-round, and two more dead in the coaster car. The surveillance film showed the vigilante methodically killed the four, then returned to find the remaining Boxby halfway over the cyclone fence.

"It appears his right shoe lace got tangled with the barbed wire that caps the fence top, " said Alexis, "He couldn't get down."

"It looks like the vigilante shot him down," said agent Kingsley staring at the fuzzy video, "You can see the body lurch."

QUANTUM ROOTS II

"The boy fell on the street side of the fence," said Alexis who used a pointer to tap the screen, "But we can see a foot just above the plastic slats. Virtually, the body is hanging by a shoelace."

"Damn," cried agent Carlson as the jumpy film rolled on, "The vigilante just shot away the shoelace."

"Hell of a shot," whistled firearms expect, agent Swiggert.

"Where did the boy get the white flag?" asked agent Spicer.

"That's his tee shirt," replied Alexis Grumman, "Take notice that his jacket is on the ground. He took off something black to get to something white."

"You are not supposed to shoot a man waving a white flag," said agent Reuben Goldberg, back from the Men's room.

"I'll mention that to the vigilante when we catch him," said Alexis.

"Why did the vigilante save that one brother for his last kill?" asked agent Kilmore from Miami.

"We don't know," replied Alexis, "Nor do we know how the vigilante happened to show up at this park."

Alexis, I'm still trapped in this revolving door, text -ed Jeremy to Alexis Grumman's cell phone.

KYLE KEYES

Sit tight, Jeremy, text ed back Alexis, *Stanley called. . . Maintenance is on their way over.*

Continued Alexis talking to the room, "Doug, run the next film, and heads up everybody. You're about to view a real *Silver Dollar Story."*

Darren and Andrea Dennis married on a joy ride hotter than a lightning strike. Andrea loved Darren's British accent and toothy smile. Darren tumbled for Andrea's *coke bottle* body form. Soon, Andrea's roving eye and Darren's jealousy surfaced. Numerous beatings and one child later, Andrea got a restraining order served on Darren. After which, she went home to mother, while Darren told every bartender in town that Andrea was just a cheap cheat.

"Doug, show the happy couple side by side," said Alexis who then pointed out Andrea's facial bruises and Darren's missing teeth in a current photo. Continued Alexis, "Andrea was about to leave this Dansville strip mall when angry husband collided with desperate carjacker."

Timing, truly can be everything. Plaza activity bustled with shoppers, pushy motorists, and the usual lunch crowd heading for a salad oriented cafeteria. The unseen carjacker saw mother and baby as a ready made target. A disoriented beer truck blocked the front entrance. A phone text told Andrea Dennis that Darren Dennis was about to ignore the restraining order. She quickly strapped in the baby and turned to grab her groceries when the assailant came from nowhere. The husky white male punched Andrea and grabbed her car keys all in one motion. Woman and hankie wipes went sprawling over cold macadam, as carjacker squealed wheels – baby still inside the silver compact.

Andrea came up screaming.

Heads turned.

A cart boy dialed 911.

"Here's where the story gets better," said Alexis pointing to the beer truck on the big screen, "With the front entrance blocked, motorists are left with two side entrances. Somehow, the carjacker and Darren Dennis came bumper to bumper at the same side entrance. We have a bedside statement from Mr. Dennis which states that he recognized the silver compact. He saw his baby inside the car. However, he mistook the carjacker for his wife's boyfriend, and that's when the scales of justice began to balance."

The two men came jaw to jaw over a smiley face stuck atop a yellow speed bump. Darren Dennis vocally unloaded on the carjacker with threats and accusations. The carjacker cut through the obscenities with a blow to Darren's solar plexus, followed by an uppercut that took out Darren's teeth and sent him hospital bound with a severe head concussion.

"County General tells us he's lucky to be alive," said Alexis, "Good news for Darren, bad news for the boyfriend."

"What do we have on this boyfriend?" asked agent Spicer,

"We have nothing," replied Alexis, "This is the Department For Paranormal Activities. Infidelity is not a strange event."

Chuckles broke out.

Alexis, where are those maintenance guys?

Not now, Jeremy.

Continued Alexis looking from cell phone to wall screen, "With two exits blocked, our carjacker speeds toward the service entrance, only to come face to face with the vigilante. Black hat. Legs spread apart. Gun hand inches from a leg holster."

"What's he doing in Dansville?" asked agent Carlson.

"We don't know," replied Alexis.

"Why is sunlight gleaming off a badge?"

"We can only guess," said Alexis, "Perhaps, he believes himself to be a lawman."

QUANTUM ROOTS II

The carjacker floored the gas pedal. The vigilante drew and began firing. The front bumper dropped as both tires blew. The bumper caught a speed riser and the silver compact flipped onto it's roof and slid toward the vigilante, who pulled the baby from the wreckage just before the car exploded.

"So now our vigilante is a hero," said CIA agent Spicer.

"Social media thinks so," replied Alexis, "*Like* clicks went wild. Press and TV reporters are struggling to stay unbiased. Other polls are not in yet."

"The carjacker is burning alive," cried Agent Goldberg turning eye and ear away from silent screams coming from the film," Why doesn't he get out?"

"He's trapped in the seat belt," said Alexis.

"Horrors!" cried Goldberg.

"Ma'am, you can not blow out a tire that quick with pistol shots," said Agent Swiggert, "The bullets would have to hit the sidewalls and not the treads."

"The vigilante did not shoot into the wheels," explained Alexis, "Our firearms expect tells us that the bullets hit the tires where rubber meets the road, and consequently blew a gaping hole in each tread. It could have been hollow points. It could have been some kind of armor-piercing, shells. We don't know."

"Hell of a shot," whistled agent Kingsley," What caused the tank to explode?"

"A ruptured gas line," explained Alexis, "Will someone get agent Goldberg a wet rag for his forehead and Doug, back the film up to where carjacker drops husband."

Arrogance can often bite us in the ass. Darren Davis lie unconscious on the parking lot. Andrea Davis had yet to reach the car. The carjacker could have just driven away. Instead, he elected to light a cigarette and strap on a seat belt. Then as the baby's mother neared the car, he flashed the middle finger, and laughingly peeled wheels. Minutes later, the cigarette would ignite the gas tank.

"If you look close," said Alexis tapping the big screen with a pointer, "You can see a small stream of gasoline leaking into the drivers' area. The disoriented carjacker never did find the seat belt button."

"Why does the vigilante think he's a lawman," asked Special Agent Carlson.

"I smell flesh burning," moaned Agent Gold-
-berg sneaking peeks at graphic screen images, "I hate that smell. I remember when our Dalmatian got run over by a fire truck. Father burned the dog in our back-yard barbecue to save cremation fees."

QUANTUM ROOTS II

Alexis Grumman stared long and hard at Reuben Goldberg before returning to agent Carlson's question. The answer lie in files from two years back. She began with photos of Olan Chapman and Jesse Joe Jacks, who was dubbed The Vigilante by wire services and social media, everywhere. Oddly enough, Chapman and Jacks were born fifty years apart, but bore identical finger-prints. Thus, the case wound up with Alexis Grumman and the Department For Paranormal Activities.

Continued Alexis, "And fingerprints is where the similarity ends. Jacks came home from Korea as a war hero, while Chapman once led an anti-gun protest just outside of Buffalo City. Jacks loved nature and died from a lightning bolt in 1959. Chapman drank too much and went over Niagara Falls in a motor boat, two years ago."

"But both men did play the piano," called out a voice from behind the scenes, "Also, their bodies were never found."

"Yes Doug," conceded Alexis, "Both men were accomplished organists as well – and neither body was ever found. Also, both men had a compassion for lower animal species."

"Jacks appears to be taller than Chapman," said Agent Spicer studying the big screen.

"He wears boot lifts," explained Alexis, "He also vanished wearing a deputy badge."

"Well, that answers my question as to why the vigilante wears a badge," said Agent Carlson,

"Not so fast," replied Alexis, "We have no evidence that Jacks is our current vigilante. We have no fingerprints, and our film clips are from the rear, We do have proof that his alter ego went over the Falls. Run the Niagara tape, Doug."

The archive film showed that Olan Chapman was halfway between the Gill Creek delta and Goat Island when pursuing helicopters closed in on his 16 HP outboard. Niagara Falls lie dead ahead. Local lawmen lined Goat Island's coastline from Three Sisters Island to Terrapin Point.

"The choppers are federal," said Alexis, "They worked for me at the time."

The twin helicopters could do little but helplessly circle the Niagara River, as the tiny outboard churned toward the point of no return. When Chapman reached Goat Island, he veered to the Canadian side and headed toward the thundering Falls.

"This guy is nuts," said Agent Spicer.

"Olan Chapman is possibly suicidal," said Alexis, "Jacks was his alter-ego. However, Jacks is a veteran survivor, which only magnifies our dilemma and returns the case to this department. Now, watch closely and you will see a third helicopter join the fracas. This chopper turned out to be a home grown swat team, armed with rifles and a police radio."

The swat team fired at the motor boat. Olan fired back. The third helicopter exploded in mid-air. Federal guns then opened fire on Olan - just as the tiny craft went over the falls.

"I don't believe Chapman could have shot that chopper out of the air," said Agent Kingsley.

"He didn't," said Alexis, "When we recovered Olan Chapman's ammo belt, the shells turned out to be blanks. The real shooter used a high powered rifle, and fired from some point on shore."

"I take it we found the shooter?"

"No we didn't," replied Alexis, "We believe the shot came from a foreign source, gunning for one of our agents."

"Well," said Agent Spicer, "I'm convinced that Jacks and Chapman are dead, which suggests we are looking for a copy cat vigilante."

"Which is why I wanted you gentlemen to view this film," said Alexis, "And we need to put that word vigilante in the plural tense. Suddenly, everybody wants to be a gunfighter. Every quack out there looking for attention is strapping on a firearm. Maybe it's a sign of the times. Anyway, we have more sightings than agents. Consequently, I can only assign one agent per sighting. Texas has a motto – one riot, one ranger. Our current slogan will be – one sighting, one soldier. Marcie has your assignments. You can pick them up on your way out."

The Department For Paranormal Activities grew gradually silent as agents wrapped up small talk and faded off. The invisible Doug shut down the big screen, but left on the monitors that interfaced with the second floor, operations room. Alexis removed the cold water press from Goldberg's forehead, and draped the folded towel over an oval conference table. She gave the junior agent a long moment stare. She removed a frayed membership card from her uniform jacket and queried,

"How long have you had this bladder infection."

"Actually, I have Colitis," said Goldberg.

"You know where The Club is ?"

Agent Goldberg nodded.

"Of course you do," said Alexis, "Take this card and tell Henry to mix you up something to calm the bowels - and put it on my tab."

"I'm not allowed any dairy products."

QUANTUM ROOTS II

"Henry won't give you any milk."

"Yes Ma'am."

"And Goldberg -

 "Yes Ma'am?"

"Gym in the morning."

"Yes Ma'am."

*   *   *   *   *

Alexis just left DPA headquarters when her two-way signaled an incoming text.

Boss, I'm out of the revolving door.

Meeting's over, Jeremy.

You're pissed.

I'm not pissed, text ed Alexis, *and FYI, you are headed for White Plains NY.*

What's up, Alexis?

We're on duty, Jeremy."

Yes boss, so what's up?

I want you to cover a vigilante sighting..

Are we traveling together, boss ?

No, I'm headed for the detention center.

Well, I hope the motor pool is still open.

No car, Jeremy.

Alexis!

KYLE KEYES

Jeremy, you drove that last car off a cliff into a gravel hole. And one other thing, you don't confide to Stanley The Doorman that I like it on top.

Chapter 3

Heavy rains pounded the prison grounds as Lt General Alexis Grumman ran from the chopper to the rooftop entrance of the Lower Elk County, Correction Center – formerly, the Mt Loyal City Jail. This South Jersey prison looms along the muddy banks of South Branch Creek, and is home to many a homeless who are away from home. Cells are crowded, beds a premium. Occasionally, waves of gleeful inmates go free to make room for society hard cores. The phrase *lockdown* is a household word. Guards patrol in battle groups. Playgrounds, libraries and workshops give an illusion of rehabilitation, but only the back waters run untroubled. Even the warden wants out.

Alexis took the elevator to the ground floor. Gun and guards stood everywhere. A wall plaque dedicated the building *to Lt Emmet Walker Thomas*. The honor was in memory of a black county detective who solved a high end murder case: code name – *The Pandarus File*. Alexis paused to read the inscription. Her youthful coworker, Jeremy Wade had worked that case before transferring to the DPA – with Alexis pulling the right strings.   She found the main lobby, and flashed her credentials to a fat desk sergeant who quickly scanned a computer screen before saying, "Yes, we've got her here."

"Thank god," said Alexis, "I thought maybe we lost her."

"Nobody's really lost, General," said the guard with a bored smile, "Everybody's in the system some-where."

"I'm sure," said Alexis, "But this *somebody* was supposed to be in New York State. How did she wind up down here, in Lower Elk County?"

"Computer error or cell space," said the guard, "The bad guys are multiplying faster than bed count . . . you want her brought down to the visitor's room?"

"I'll see her where she is," said Alexis.

"Our accommodations are up to code," assured the desk sergeant.

"I'm not from civil liberties," said Alexis.

"We need to check your briefcase," said the desk sergeant.

"Of course," replied Alexis.

"Just doing my job."

"I understand, Sergeant."

QUANTUM ROOTS II

Tiny cells ran two levels high in this stone and steel structure, funded on a skimpy county budget. Fluorescent light fixtures designed for three bulbs, held two bulbs only. Ceiling fans kept the power bill down. Whistles and lewd remarks followed Alexis Grumman's noisy heels down the male corridor that led to female quarters. A stocky matron unlocked an electronic door that opened into the smaller east wing. Rosemary Gondolas Mendez sat on a cot in the last cell on ground level. She wore gray prison garb, her brown locks tied in a bun. Tattoos covered one arm, and ran down one leg like so many islands on an ocean map. She mumbled a greeting without looking up.

"Where's her street clothes?" asked Alexis.

"In a locker," replied the stocky matron.

"She's supposed to be here as a detainee."

"She bit me in the arm," said the matron, "And since you forewent the visitor's checkpoint, I'm required to wait."

"No privacy needed," replied Alexis turning her questions to the Cuban porn queen.

"I don't know where Romano es hiding," said Rosemary Mendez, "I have already told the police all I know. We were shooting a movie. It was only a film."

"A porn film?" asked Alexis for verification.

"Yes, porn film for Havana," replied Rosemary.

"Why were you shooting the film stateside?"

"You'll have to ask Romano."

"Why did you lie about the gang rape?" asked Alexis.

"My interrogator was salivating," replied the Cuban porn queen, "I told the pig what he wanted to hear."

"We are sending you home," said Alexis playing a little *good cop, bad cop*, "You must miss Havana. We all miss home when away from home."

"I miss my cigarettes."

Alexis opened the briefcase and extracted all the photographs the FIC had on the vigilante. Some were fuzzy, some dark. One or two were sunlight clear. Said Alexis, "We need a positive ID on the shooter. Right now we only have weapon caliber to tie this shooting to other vigilante shootings."

"It was dark," said Rosemary Mendez.

"You must have seen something."

"I saw gunfire."

"We know that your cousin Romano filmed the attack and maybe some of the fireworks," said Alexis, "Did he by chance catch the shooter on film?"

"I do not know," said Rosemary.

QUANTUM ROOTS II

"Could this be the man who shot your cousin Chico Mendez," asked Alexis tapping a full size picture of the vigilante, "This photo was taken at the Dansville Shopping Center, by a teenager with a cell phone. We had it blown up. It clearly shows the vigilante to be a right-handed gun. Two years back, our vigilante was left-handed. You can see our dilemma. Can you help us with this?"

The Cuban porn queen shrugged. A loose bun comb fell to the concrete floor as she studied the photograph. Her makeup was two days old. She had a broken fingernail from her admittance altercation. A stomach knot now had her bowels off cycle. She glared at the stocky matron and then said to Alexis, "I cannot help you."

"Think back," prompted Alexis, "Did this gunman shoot from the right side or the left side, you must remember that."

"He stood in the shadows," said Rosemary, "I could only hear the gun."

"Did you see Chico throw the knife?" asked Alexis.

"It was a rubber knife."

"Yes," acknowledged Alexis.

"It was just a prop."

"Your statement to local police claims that the gunman shot the rubber knife out of the air."

"Yes," confirmed the porn queen.

"Then, you must have seen the vigilante shoot this prop out of the air," said Alexis.

"My Chico was unarmed," spit Rosemary, "This vigilante es the one who belongs in jail, not me."

Changing direction, Alexis pulled another picture enlargement from her open briefcase. The photograph showed the back alley steps that led to the balcony where Romano shot the porno film. Said Alexis, "The door that opens into the apartment is boarded over. So we know that Romano Mendez used the steps to exit the crime scene. We also know the authorities found you kneeing next to your cousin, Chico Mendez. Which means. . . . cousin Romano had to pass right by you and Chico to exit the alley."

"I loved Chico," said Rosemary.

"I'm sure you did," said Alexis, "However, you and cousin Romano must have spoke."

"Romano chose to film here," said Rosemary Mendez, "I wanted to film in Havana."

"Yes, we've been over that," said Alexis growing impatient, "But Romano must have given you contact information before taking off."

QUANTUM ROOTS II

"And my Chico," lamented the Cuban porn queen, "Chico wanted to film in Havana."

"I think you are holding back," said Alexis.

"Read my lips," spit Rosemary, "Cousin Romano has told me nothing."

"I was hoping you might be more helpful," said Alexis.

"I want my lawyer," said Rosemary Mendez.

"You can get a lawyer back in Cuba," said Alexis, "And let's be clear about something, Ms Mendez. You sent an innocent woman into an alley to be victimized physically and mentally, so you could get black market money for a porn film. As far as I'm concerned, the vigilante might have aimed the gun, but you pulled the trigger. Now, political pressure is sending you home, while your victim remains under a physician's care. Frankly, if this mess was on my plate, I'd have your fat ass in a court room."

*   *   *   *   *

Heavy rain continued as Alexis ducked under swirling blades to re board the chopper. She dropped the briefcase between the seats, and dried off her hair with a oil stained, maintenance towel.

"Ma'am, I couldn't help but notice when you boarded," said Pilot Richard Kramer with a hesitant draw, "But you have a great set of legs."

"Thank you Lieutenant," said Alexis, "I already have a male companion."

"Just my luck."

"And Lieutenant?"

"Yes Ma'am?"

"If I might say this without stepping on Colonel Swan's toes, I want that hair cut. You're a federal agent, Kramer. You are not Jesus Christ."

"Yes Ma'am."

Alexis flipped open her classified cell phone, and text ed, *Jeremy, are you in White Plains, yet?*

Just pulling in.

Good, Why was you communicator off ?

I had it in the charger.

Don't bullshit me, Jeremy.

Ut oh, somebody's still pissed.

I'm not pissed,

Whatever you say, Alexis.

Just keep me updated and don't call me Alexis while we are on duty.

Yes, boss.

And Jeremy?

QUANTUM ROOTS II

Yes Ma'am ?

I received a text from General Taylor. You are on report for crushing the plants in the front planter back at headquarters.

Reported by who?

Reported by Stanley.

Alexis, there aren't any plants in that planter !

And one other thing, Jeremy.

Listening.

You don't confide to Stanley The Doorman that I have a tattoo on my ass.

Chapter 4

"I'm special agent, Jeremy Wade," said Jeremy Wade standing at the entrance door to the White Plains playhouse. Lilac bushes lined the front of this cobble stone building, founded before Washington crossed the Delaware. An overhead marque advertised a coming attraction called the Gray Pretenders. Bike racks divided the lilac bushes.

"I didn't know federal agents traveled by motor scooter," said the doorman staring at Wade's mode of transportation, now squeezed between a mountain bike and a three wheeler.

"Looks can be deceiving," said Jeremy.

"I've heard that," said the doorman.

"You can't judge a book by it's cover," said the special agent.

"Tell me something I don't know," said the door man.

Jeremy Wade picked up the fallen scooter and pointed to the odometer, "This baby can actually out run the speed of sound."

QUANTUM ROOTS II

"You are kidding," said the doorman.

"Forge a raging river," said Jeremy.

"Wow!" said the doorman.

"Sail over stalled traffic."

"I think it just fell over," said the doorman.

"The kickstand's broken," said Jeremy.

"I'll show you the manager," said the doorman.

The ancient playhouse hosted concerts, showed movies and catered to any theatrical group who wished to stage a Broadway musical. Velvet lined chairs ran in three sections from the front lobby to a panoramic stage, flooded by overhead spotlights. Varnished side walls lined the carpeted aisles. Refreshments were purchased just inside the entrance doors

"There's no business like show business, like no business I know," said Jeremy Wade.

"You have been in show business?" queried Arnold Swedlow who was owner, manager and money counter for this curbside establishment, run on ticket sales and nostalgia donations.

"School plays," replied Jeremy.

"Oh," said Arnold Swedlow.

"Three years running," bubbled Jeremy, "In my senior year we did a re pro of that musical classic, *The Mensa And The Moron.* "

"I'm not familiar with that production," yawned Arnold Swedlow.

"Had a long run on Broadway," remembered Jeremy, "Very compelling plot. The story centers about a boy genius who learns early on that people don't like smart people."

"So he decides to play the part of a fool," said Swedlow, munching on popcorn.

"You have seen the play," said Jeremy.

"Lucky guess," said Swedlow.

"Anyway, I played both the boy genius and the dummy," explained Jeremy, "What a challenge. I only had fifteen seconds to make each costume change. But I did learn that the dunce hat gets accepted before the cap and gown."

In retrospect, Jeremy Wade never starred in a high school play entitled *The Mensa And The Moron,* or any other stage production, not even to pull the curtain. Nor, was there any Broadway script by any such name. *Mensa And The Moron* was in fact, Jeremy Wade's own life story. Special Agent Wade was born to Joshua and Janice Wade, who were dirt farmers from southern Ohio, corn country. Both parents were of average intelligence and could not account for their child prodigy, who never cracked a homework book, yet graduated high school at age thirteen. Ten years later, the young Wade held a master's degree in criminology, and took a twenty one week course at Quantico, VA to become an FBI special agent.

"I could use more pop corn," said Swedlow.

"I passed the vision test by memorizing the eye charts before-hand," confessed Jeremy, "I wear contacts so people won't call me *ole four eyes.*"

"We all have our cross to bear," said Swedlow, "People often refer to me as *ole chrome dome.*"

Jeremy, could we get back to the business of tracking down the vigilante., text ed in Alexis

*Of course, bos*s.

When the angry gunman stormed into the White Plains playhouse, Arnold Swedlow stood but a few feet away munching on popcorn. Ticket lines were long and the concession counter, busy. Explained Swedlow, "He probably did not see me for the patrons."

"He was gunning for you?" queried Jeremy.

"I'm the one who fired him."

The shooter was a former maintenance man for this White Plains playhouse. His name was Randolph Washington Robinson. Nickname, Dandy Do. His duties included cleanup, ushering, and sometimes working the ticket office. Swedlow fired Dandy Do a week earlier for smoking pot and stealing an undetermined amount of money from the cash register. Robinson was single, self focused and self serving. He shot and killed six patrons before the vigilante put a bullet between his eyes.

"So, the popcorn saved your life," said Jeremy.

"I love popcorn," said the balding middle aged manager, "Especially loaded with butter. Here, have a bag."

"Thank you and I love your tie," said Jeremy eagerly accepting the handout.

"Bow ties are making a comeback," said Arnold Swedlow, "Good thing, too. They are less trouble than fumbling around with a conventional tie. The downside occurs when they jump around on my adam's apple."

"I guess your bow tie really jumped that night the gunman was here," suggested Jeremy.

Jeremy, you are on duty!

Yes, boss.

This matter is serious.

Sorry.

And what are you munching on?

Popcorn..

Can we get on with business?

"He just started shooting people," said Arnold Swedlow moving on with the sequence of events, "He just walked down the center aisle and opened fire. The whole place went bonkers. The agile stampeded over the crippled trying to get out the exits.

"Horrific for sure," said Jeremy.

"I did not know he carried a grudge," said the manager, referring to the shooter, "I did not know he carried a gun, and I did not know he was that pissed."

He made no threats after being fired? text ed in Alexis.

"Nary a one," replied Swedlow to the text.

The real sick ones often don't, said Alexis,

"The real sick ones don't," echoed Jeremy

Jeremy put me on the speaker phone !

"I'm putting my boss on the speaker phone," said Jeremy Wade while fumbling with the two-way.

"Mr Swedlow, this is Alexis Grumman," said the lady general, "I'm director for the division of para-normal activities. When did you first see the vigilante?"

"When the curtain opened for Act Three," said the manager, "We were doing a stage production of Annie Get You Gun, only it was this vigilante guy who showed up with the gun. As the intruder reloaded his pistol, he saw the vigilante and swung his gun toward the stage. Tee Vee style. Both hands on the pistol, extended at arm's length. He looked like he was sniffing his own armpit."

"And the vigilante?" asked Alexis.

"He shot from the hip," replied Swedlow now standing at a chalky outline where the intruder died, "Don't know how I'm going to get these blood stains out. I'll probably have to purchase new carpeting."

"How did the vigilante get on stage?" asked the lady general.

"Beats me," said the manager, "The only people who belonged on stage was the cast and Benny."

"Who's Benny?" asked Alexis.

"He's our newest crew member," replied Arnold Swedlow, "I hired him to take Robinson's place."

"He was an usher?"

"Among other things," said Swedlow.

"Why would an usher be on the stage?" asked Alexis.

"He was on piano," replied the manager.

The classified communicator went momentarily silent. Jeremy Wade stopped munching popcorn as he stared intently at Arnold Swedlow. Cried Alexis, "This new man was also your piano player!"

"He filled in for our piano player," explained the manager, "Our regular pianist went home ill and Benny took his place. Funny thing though, Benny was better than Norman – that's our regular pianist.'

Jeremy, show him a photo of Olan Chapman !

"I can't be sure," said Swedlow peeking at the photo on Jeremy Wade's two-way, "He has the same lip mole but I just can't be sure."

A stocky woman wih a goose feather in a giant hat, entered the hall. She spotted Arnold Swedlow and began waving flabby arms wildly She was president of the ladies Crazy Hat Club. She had an appointment with Swedlow to cancel the club's upcoming stage drama entitled, HATS OFF TO LARRY. Said Jeremy upon the manager's return, "We need to talk to this guy."

"Larry's just a guy in a song," said Swedlow.

"We need to talk to Benny," said Jeremy.

"People are canceling left and right," lamented Swedlow, "This shooting will ruin my business."

"Mister Swedlow, this is Lt General Grumman," said Alexis over the open speaker line, "We need to talk to this piano player."

"Can't," said Arnold Swedlow.

"Can't?"

"He and the vigilante disappeared at the same time."

"He left without being paid?" asked Alexis.

"Yes ma'am."

"Did he leave anything behind?"

"No ma'am," replied Arnold Swedlow, "Came here with a backpack, left with a backpack."

"You saw him leave?" asked Alexis.

"No, but the backpack's gone," replied Arnold Swedlow, "Robinson lived off the grounds, but I gave Benny a room in the back. It's still roped off."

Jeremy, keep the room roped off and then return to headquarters. I'm sending our forensic team up there.

Jeremy Wade paused outside the White Plains playhouse to receive another text message from Alexis Grumman. The junior agent re-entered the building and then returned to the scooter where he text ed back: *Alexis, we do have an issue here.*

Listening, replied the female director.

The manager remembers this vigilante as being right-handed.

He's sure, Jeremy ?

He remembers the gun firing from the balcony side, which puts the gun in the vigilante's right hand.

But Jeremy, Jesse Joe Jacks was left handed.

Agent Jeremy Wade stood the scooter upright, and wiped down the black seat, wet from a wayward water sprinkler. He poured water from a matching black helmet. He sighed, and flipped open his communicator. to text, *Jacks was left handed* for sure . . .*So who are we looking for, boss?*

"Yes," mused General Alexis Grumman, staring at the big screen back at headquarters, while muttering aloud, "Who in the hell are we looking for?"

Chapter 5

Dateline: April, 1876

Deputy Marshal, Leroy McCoy strode past the dry goods shop and Hoovers Cigar Store. Rolling dust balls blew down the dirt street and past watchful horses tied to hitching posts. A blacksmith hammer beat out a metallic rhythm just off Main Street. McCoy paused to finger the Colt 45 strapped to his lower right leg, then the slender lawman burst into the Long Branch Saloon. He looked like an dusty rodeo rider thrown from a mad bull, just out of the gate.

All fell silent in this busy Dodge City barroom. The piano player who had been ordered to keep playing, stopped playing. Dancing girls told to keep dancing, stopped dancing. Table whispers became a hush, as the three holdup men turned their focus from the open cash register, to the stony lawman silhouetted just inside the swinging doors.

"Holster your hardware," demanded McCoy, who had been alerted by a barefooted newsboy, that a robbery was in progress, "You're under arrest."

QUANTUM ROOTS II

The three holdup men were widely known as the Ghost Riders. They had fled Wichita and invaded this boom town dubbed Dodge City, founded to serve the influx of cattle drives along the Chisholm Trail. The Civil War over, America forged ahead by moving cattle by rail to eastern markets. Expansion towns like Dodge City were now in the lime light, and stockyards bulged with cattle trade numbers that ran into the thousands. There was a downside to this *money merry-go-round*. Often, greed will follow growth, spawning drifters, highway men and cold blooded killers.

"Throw down our hardware?" sneered Billy Bob Thurston who was gang leader for the Ghost Riders, and accustomed to giving orders, not taking them, "Who the hell are you?'

"You only get one warning from me," flatly said Leroy McCoy who had yet to draw a weapon.

"I gotta bead on him," whispered little brother Bobo to big brother Billy.

"I gotta bead on him, too," said the third gun man, who was also named Bobo because the two boys were twins. Their parents had selected the name from a circus banner back East, and were unprepared for the double blessing. Years later, the blessing turned tainted when the twins headed west to find fame and fortune.

KYLE   KEYES

"You were told to lift wallets and watches," said brother Billy, "I'll handle Johnny Law."

"But I can take him," cried Bobo One taking his gun sight off a faro dealer hiding behind a handlebar mustache.

"Let me drop him," begged Bobo Two, "I need a notch on this new gun I got."

McCoy's steady eyes surveyed the situation. The twins appeared to be the weak link. Their talk came off brazen, but their gun barrels quivered. Clearly, Billy Bob was the would-be threat. Reputation traveled ahead of frontier gunslingers, and the older Thurston brother wanted his name, Billy Bob to be feared throughout the West, grab East Coast headlines, and rival such legends as Jesse James, Tom and Frank McLaury, Ike and Billy Clanton, etc.

"Time's up," said Leroy McCoy.

Old West gun fighters would often tip their hand with a finger twitch or eye blink. In this case, it was the eye blink that did in Billy Bob Thurston. McCoy picked up the blink and fired off three rounds with a draw so quick, no one saw his hand move. The first shot hit Billy Bob square between the eyes. Blood squirted onto the sandy plank floor of this recently built saloon. The second bullet caught the first Bobo with his mouth open, and blew away some rotted teeth. The third shot left McCoy's Colt 45 as the final brother managed to squeeze off a round. The two blasts sounded like one gun shot. Both men slumped to the floor with chest wounds.

Stunned silence came first. Then Walter the barkeep came from behind the counter and rushed to the fallen bodies.

The final Thurston brother lie dead.

Leroy McCoy still breathed.

Cried Walter, "Somebody get Doc Sweeney."

*   *   *   *   *

"Well, if you ain't just about luckier than a dog with two peckers," said Willard Sweeney MD kneeling over the fallen body of Leroy McCoy. The bullet fired by Bobo Thurston had pierced a silver dollar hanging from McCoy's neck. The coin took most of the fire power force, which left the bullet slightly lodged in McCoy's breast bone. Later, fixing hot water and clean towels back in his doctor's office, Sweeney said, "Digging this out will hurt a bit."

"Sure nuff," replied Leroy McCoy.

"Should I strap you down?" asked Sweeney.

KYLE KEYES

"Just git on with it," growled McCoy swigging whiskey used as an anesthetic, "I've endured worse."

"You're new here," said the Dodge City medic, "Who hired you anyway?"

"City marshal over in Wichita deputized me," replied McCoy, "The Thurstons robbed a Sante Fe construction camp and vanished without a hoof print. Council needed a good tracker with a fast gun, so the marshal put a badge on me."

"Gun fighter, eh?"

"Bounty hunter by trade," replied McCoy, "Fill in as a lawman when needed."

"Earp is due here next month," said Sweeney stroking a giant mustache as he peered over tiny eye glasses,

"Wyatt ?"

"The same."

At this point in time, Wyatt Berry Stapp Earp was a deputy city marshal in Wichita, Kansas. Earp officially joined the marshal's office on April 21, 1875. He wore a cloth badge and carried a Colt 45 to neutralize drunken trail cowboys. Wyatt's job ended abruptly on April 2, 1876, when Police Chief Mike Meagher fired Wyatt on charges of nepotism – namely, using his office to hire brothers, Virgil and James as deputies. After which, Earp followed James to Dodge city, where Marshall Lawrence Deger appointed Wyatt Earp as assistant marshal.

"I'll be back in Wichita with three dead bodies by the time Wyatt gets here," said McCoy pulling on boots and grimacing from chest bandages, "I got some money coming to me. You might say it's a trade-off. Wyatt's coming to Dodge, and I'm heading for Wichita."

"You want this slug?"

"I'll take my lucky dollar," replied McCoy.

Chapter 6

Dateline: Today

Alexis Grumman and Jeremy Wade sat trading eye talk in a window booth at *Nickles Bar And Grille.* Outside, black clouds signaled an oncoming storm. Inside, whiskey driven threats from the noisy bar grew louder – and louder.

"I sense trouble brewing,"   said Alexis.

"No worries,"   replied Jeremy,   "I'm armed."

"That's what worries me."

Nickles is a back street pub located just off the Eastern By Pass, and not far from F.I.C. Headquarters. This ever popular hangout boasts a full service bar and televises all football games, collegiate, high school and professional. *Nickles* also has a hot spot for computer freaks, nerds and white collar investors. Dinner prices are reasonable and discretion is the door key. Alexis and Jeremy liked it here because it kept department gossip down. Truth was, the *cougar* talk bothered the youthful Jeremy more so than the older Alexis. The female general spent much of her twenty year career in third world countries, where life holds less value than here in the land of stars and stripes. Thus, Alexis flew under a banner that read, *Life Is Short, Grab All The Tail You Can.* Said Alexis while munching on a spinach salad, "Have you ever shot anybody?"

"Does pepper spray count?"

"That's what I thought," said Alexis as two bar stool voices resorted to the F word.

"You won't believe this," said Jeremy, "When I worked out of global tracking, we had an adage – *One agent equals one army.*"

Alexis put a finger to Jeremy Wade's lips as two marines from nearby Quantico carried verbal threats into a shoving match, and were now tossing a wayward sailor back and forth like a rag doll. Tony the bartender was first to intervene, only to be shoved back behind the bar. Then, Frankie the bouncer crumbled from a jaw breaking right cross, which brought Jeremy Wade to his feet.

"I'm Federal Agent, Jeremy Wade," said Jeremy Wade talking over rolling thunder from outside.

"And I'm Mr Peepers," laughed a marine larger than a dump truck.

"Let the sailor go," ordered Jeremy in some-what lower tones.

KYLE KEYES

"Up your ass," sneered the marine tossing the sailor back to the other marine.

"I can get you booted out of the service," said Jeremy Wade,

"They're already on a Section Eight," said Tony the bartender, "They just got out of the brig and are supposed to be heading home to the Bijou."

"Well, I can make that happen," said Alexis with cell phone in hand, "And. . we need to get security out here fast."

Not all explosions require dynamite. Some blasts come from well aimed four letter words. In this case it was a five letter word that lit the fuse. The hefty marine called Alexis a *bitch*, which swung Jeremy into action. The slender agent plowed into the giant marine, who grabbed Jeremy by the hair with one hand, as he held the sailor with the other hand.

The crowd went crazy.

"So which one gets to play ping pong," hooted the giant marine.

"Let's go with the sailor boy," cried the smaller marine, "I hate these gobs. It was the navy who let my cousin drown in the Mojave Ocean."

"Pinky," growled the first marine, "The Mojave is a desert."

QUANTUM ROOTS II

"Whatever," replied the smaller marine, "I say we sink the navy."

The patrons made the decision. They gave the sailor a thumbs up, and Jeremy a thumbs down. Jeremy would be the ping pong ball.

"I have the authorities coming!" warned Alexis as Jeremy stumbled from marine to marine, "Right now you two are guilty of assaulting a federal agent. Don't make it worse."

"A federal agent," cried the one marine, "Hear that Pinky, we got us a G man. We has gutted a few hogs back on the mountain, but we has never gutted us a real live G man."

Suddenly, all went quiet as the burly, attacker brandished a modified Bowie knife. The silver blade flashed under neon lights. Top and bottom were honed for skinning and thrusting. The wooden hock had been carved for knife throwing.

The marine named Pinky readied Jeremy Wade for a final push toward the menacing knife point. Patrons held a collective breath. Alexis screamed a final warning as Frankie the bouncer took another kick to the ribs.

Then, yesteryear collided with today.

The vigilante stood in the doorway.

KYLE KEYES

Feet spread.

Hands dangling loose at his side.

Eerie wind gusts whipped street dust around his black boots. Lightning flashed. An overhead thunder clap shook the building to sound nature's time clock, and would later spawn rumors that this strange visitor came via the storm from yesteryear's Dodge City.

"Who the hell are you?" sneered the massive marine holding the knife.

"This must be Wyatt Earp," laughed Pinky.

"Leroy McCoy, assistant deputy marshal," came the steady reply from beneath the black stetson with the flat brim.

"*Swat Team Leader,*" text ed Alexis Grumman into her classified two-way, "*He's here, right under our nose.*"

"*Who?*"

"*The vigilante!*"

"*Holy shit General, where are you?*"

"*Nickles.*"

"*The bar?*"

"*Yes, the bar!!!*"

"*We are on our way.*"

"Leroy McCoy!" scoffed the marine talking to the vigilante, "How 'bout I take that badge and shove it up your ass !"

The vigilante parted a black frontier coat to reveal a low slung, Colt 45. His right hand steadied the open holster. His left fore finger rubbed a handlebar mustache as he sized up the man who held Jeremy Wade in a hammerlock. Said McCoy, "Let him go."

"Let him go?"

"Let him go."

The marine holding the knife began to laugh, a nervous ripple that grew into a forced rumble, and then exploded into a full blown belly roar. Gradually, the laugh ran dry, as the giant marine realized he was the one now on the spot. This stranger was calling him out. All eyes were watching.

"Be smart and git while the gittin's good," said the giant marine, "This ain't your fight."

"Last chance," said Leroy McCoy.

The marine growled like a cornered animal. He looked from the vigilante, to Pinky, to the waiting crowd. Suddenly, he spun and hurled the flashing blade at Leroy McCoy – a deadly missile in quiet flight.

Alexis gasped.

Spectators froze.

The vigilante drew and fired three shots.

The first bullet took out the knife. The second

round caught the marine between the eyes. The third shot entered Pinky's left ear and exited from the right ear.

Blood shot out.

Gasps set in.

Then came screams, as reality ruled.

Swat team leader, this is General Grumman.

This is Swat Team Leader, over

Where the hell are you guys !

Now free from Pinky's arm lock, Jeremy Wade crumpled to the floor. Tony the bartender grabbed the house phone. Patrons ran for exit doors. Alexis ran to help Jeremy back to his feet.

The vigilante vanished.

We are here, General, came a text from Swat Leader One, *Update situation inside.*

Alexis checked Jeremy over for fractured bones and broken teeth. Finding nothing wrong but shortage of breath due to a gut punch, she text ed back to Swat Leader One, *Threat neutralized.*

Minutes later, swat team members stormed into the building, followed up by EMS and some body bags. After which, the world as we know it descended upon Nickles Bar and Grille. Alexis Grumman gave a hurried account to local authorities and press reporters, as bodies moved out, and forensics moved in. Later, she and Jeremy regained composure over a stiff drink back at Alexis' one bedroom suite.

"He appeared with that last lightning bolt," said Jeremy referring to Marshall Leroy McCoy.

"You think he came out of a lightning bolt?"

"Maybe some kind of worm hole," replied the junior agent, "He did look like an image from the early west."

"I don't believe in wormholes," said Alexis, flatly dismissing such a wild notion, "Also, I don't believe in coincidence. There has to be another answer as to why this guy showed up where we were., and how did he know we were there?"

"There's always an answer," said Jeremy staring out the fifth floor window at the Eastern Bypass traffic. An eighteen wheeler raced southbound toward county lines with a black and white in *hot pursuit*. You could see the flashing lights and faintly hear the sirens. Soon, the trucker gave in to the trooper and pulled the rig over.

"Maybe he's tracking us," said Alexis referring to the vigilante.

"Why would he be tracking us?" asked Jeremy.

"Because we're tracking him."

KYLE KEYES

"How would he know that," said Jeremy.

"I don't know," replied Alexis, "But I did hear a horse ninny."

'I'm happy to hear that," said the junior agent, "I have been researching worm holes as a possibility to negate conventional time and space travel. They are not as far fetched as you might think."

"Jeremy, I think we could use another drink."

"A wormhole is suggested by Einstein's theory of general relativity," continued Jeremy, "Also known as the Einstein-Rosen bridge, this hypothetical topological feature could be a shortcut connecting two separate points in space/time."

"Jeremy, I hope you're not taking off on one of your flights of fantasy."

"Nathan Rosen didn't think space/time points were flights of fantasy."

"I don't know any Nathan Rosen and this drink needs some more rum," said Alexis.

Nathan Rosen was a Brooklyn NY, born physicist, credited for the Einstein-Rosen bridge theory that could connect universes, time spans and space distances from a meter to points unknown. The theory first surfaced in 1921 via German mathematician, Hermann Weyl in a detailed study of electromagnetic field energy. It was later nicknamed *wormhole* by American physicist, John Archibald Wheeler in 1957.

Nathan Rosen's wormhole theory resulted from a mathematical solution for connecting distant areas in space. Working with Albert Einstein's field equations, Rosen and Einstein managed to merge mathematical models of a black hole and a white hole (a black hole moving backward in time.) The result opened the door to sci-fi theories that some physicists believe credible, while others coin as unstable.

"Well, I think it's all illusion," murmured Alexis, still pondering how and why this vigilante appeared at Nickles Bar & Grille, "It's just magic and magic always turns out to be illusion."

"Magic?"

"Yes, magic," replied Alexis.

"Maybe there's some magic in the shower," said Jeremy kicking off shoes and trousers.

"I thought you would never ask," purred Alexis sipping another rum and coke, "And this better not get back to me from Stanley The Doorman."

"It won't," promised Jeremy, "Scouts honor."

Later, under the sheets and three sheets gone.

"I can't believe you were ever a Boy Scout."

"Explorer Scout, actually."

KYLE   KEYES

"That I can believe."

Memo from General James Ironhorse Taylor to Lt General Alexis Grumman: Please provide our Office Of The Interior with a detailed, type written report of the recent barroom shooting that took place at Nickles Bar And Grille. Include an explanation as to why you and special agent Jeremy Wade happened to be present. Also, include the justification for one of our federal agents to confront members of the armed services, which resulted in the death of two marines.

Please send this office a duplicate copy.

Chapter 7

The FIC pistol range lay beyond ear shot of the headquarters building, just off the Eastern Bypass in Warrenton, Va. Wolf whistles echoed from the motor pool as Alexis walked by open bay doors, and turned down a sandy trail that forks off the bumpy service road. She stumbled as high heel caught raised rock, and caught balance before going down.

"I'd be happy to catch you!" yelled a male voice from under a car lift, "Some grease marks would look good on that cute rear end."

Alexis gave the vocal mechanic a middle finger and sashayed on toward the sounds of gunfire that riddled the mid-morning air. She found Jeremy Wade and senior citizen, Bernie Miliquist facing six straw targets backed up by a steep gravel slope. The range faced north and south to keep sunrise and sunset out of the shooter's eyes. However, seasonal sun orientation had been overlooked, and both men now squinted to zero in on the target.

"I must say that agent Wade is picking up the *point shooting* technique quite quickly," said Miliquist as Alexis walked up, .

"I'd rather Jeremy didn't carry a gun," replied Alexis watching the junior agent spin drop a thirty-two into a leg holster.

"I thought all agents carried a firearm," queried Miliquist.

"Jeremy has a problem with qualification," said the lady general.

"Which is why we are here," explained Bernie Miliquist, "Agent Wade would like to become a crack shot with a firearm."

"His idea or yours?" asked Alexis, keenly aware that outside interests often milk the government for money.

"His idea," replied Miliquist.

"I will be ready for my next encounter with the vigilante," said Jeremy Wade, firmly.

"Agent Wade needs to hone his skills with a gun before he faces anyone," said Miliquist.

"Please point him down range," said Alexis.

Bernie Miliquist was a *special projects* instructor for this post 911, intelligence center. Occasionally, the F.I.C. would employ a civilian with expertise in firearms,

QUANTUM ROOTS II

karate, explosives and various forms of self defense. Miliquist specialized in handguns and a firing stance dubbed, *Point Shooting*.

Bernie Miliquist learned *Point Shooting* from a hand book written by Bobby "Lucky" McDaniel, a nine--teen fifties icon who taught fast draw and hip shooting with an air rifle. McDaniel found that slow moving BB's were visible to the naked eye, which made it possible for the student to track *hits* and *misses*. Such an aid lets the armed novice move quickly from a conventional sight picture to the mind's eye. Added Bernie Miliquist, "Many of Lucky McDaniel's students were bird hunters, target shooters and police officers of that era. Choice of gun made little difference. McDaniel could teach any one to shoot anything. Following suit, I will now move Jeremy from a thirty-two caliber, up to a thirty-eight, and then on to a forty-five."

"That holster seems very close to his penis," said Alexis.

"That holster is a modified Jordan used for fast draw, cowboy shooting," explained Miliquist, "Notice how the gun handle tilts away from the hip. This allows the shooter to lift the weapon away cleanly from the holster."

"I think he just hit a cloud," said Alexis.

KYLE KEYES

"He's not used to the forty-five," said Miliquist, "Heavier weapons can kick like a mule. The key here is to brace your firing elbow against your solar plexus. This is your horizontal sight. Now, bring your free hand over to the weapon, and use an eye and your index finger as your vertical sight. Also, your horizontal movement is executed by twisting on the balls of your feet, while your neck, waist and hips are kept locked in position. These are the keys to successful *Point Shooting*."

"I think our company is here," murmured Alexis as a distant horn sounded top brass arrival. Loose road cinders swirled about the weathered army jeep that looked like a WWII leftover. Range dust flew and brakes screeched, seconds before two men jumped to the ground. The youthful driver stood at parade rest next to an olive drab fender. The older man came boldly forward. His step was brisk. His highly decorated, jacket sparkled from overhead sunlight. Said Alexis amid a series of salutes, "Bernie, this is General James Iron-horse Taylor. . .General, this is the gentleman I told you about."

"As you can see," said General Taylor talking to General Grumman, "I haven't lost a step since retiring to the F.I.C.."

QUANTUM ROOTS II

"I can see that," said Alexis, "You could have signed out a newer jeep you know."

General James Taylor locked thumbs inside his service belt to emphasize a flat stomach, and grinned broadly to show off some new dentures that were too white for his weathered face. He wiped gravel marks off his black oxfords and went on to explain that now and then he would pretend to be back on front lines.

"Commendable," said Alexis, who knew that Taylor had no wartime record, and had seen little action but for an occasional beer garden brawl, and maybe a wayward mortar shell fired by his own troops.

"Always good to see you, Alexis."

"Likewise, general."

James Taylor's military career included peacetime tours to Germany, Korea and Vietnam, matching those service tours of Alexis Grumman. Often, their paths hit crossroads where Alexis would turn down Taylor's offers for those of younger men. Alexis would then remind the general that there was a Mrs Taylor – tactfully. Now widowed, the general was on the prowl again.

"Is this the cowboy shooter?" asked General Taylor nodding toward Bernie Miliquist.

"The same," replied Alexis with a nose to the air, "What do I smell?"

"After shave lotion," crowed the general, "As a leader of men, I like to smell like a man."

"Of course," said Alexis. Then leaning toward Bernie Miliquist, she whispered, "The general is my immediate superior. He calls hip shooting a cowboy movie stunt. Anyway, I need to show him some hard evidence that this vigilante is the real deal."

Miliquist stopped packing up a canvass tote bag. The thin gray mustache beneath his tiny nose appeared to smile as he said, "I gave you a demonstration two years back."

"You did," acknowledged Alexis Grumman.

"Will a re-run work?"

"It will."

Bernie Miliquist squared off with the first target. He stood with feet spread 18 inches apart, knees flexed. He drew without warning. Six shots rang out in three seconds. He hit all six bulls-eyes.

"Damn," cried General James Taylor.

"I intend to get that good," bubbled Jeremy.

General Taylor swung a steely gaze from down range, back to Jeremy Wade who now stood at parade rest. Taylor and Wade were not strangers. Over the past two years, the FIC director served constant disciplinary actions against Wade for numerous code infractions.

QUANTUM ROOTS II

Said Taylor, "I see your shoes are shined and your hair now conforms to military requirements, soldier."

"Yes, Sir."

"I've been on top of him," said Alexis.

"Good," boomed Taylor who then whispered to Alexis, "I discipline a lot of soldiers. I recall more faces than names. Is this the Jeremy Wade who got gored by a bull in Spain?"

"Almost gored," replied Alexis.

"The agent who stole a bystander's motorbike and crashed through a sidewalk cafe on his way to Molinos?"

"The same, Sir."

"I thought he worked out of the global tracking agency ," said General Taylor.

"Jeremy got transferred to us, Sir."

"Yes, well shit happens," muttered the general, "Just stay on top of this man."

"Yes, Sir."

"Now we move on to objects in flight," said Miliquist, regaining everyone's attention, "The key here is to practice with colored BB's so the shooter can observe flight patterns. First, shoot ahead of the target, then purposely shoot behind the target. Eventually, the subconscious mind will find the center."

The small arms instructor put away the air gun and reloaded his twenty-two. He pulled a yellow tennis ball from his tote bag. He lobbed the ball skyward with his left hand. He shot the ball out of the air with his right hand. Next, he ran the demonstration with a golf ball, then asked for a dime. He would attempt to hit the dime in mid air.

"I remember this shot," said Jeremy, "Next to impossible."

"You toss it and I'll hit it," said Bernie Miliquist who was good to his boast. Seconds later, the hip-draw specialist blew the floating coin out of the air."

"Damn!" exclaimed Jeremy, "I've seen you do this before and I still can't believe it."

"But, that's only a twenty-two," reminded the lady general steering the conversation to make a point, "The vigilante fires a Colt 45."

"Yes, what about the heavy frame weapon?" asked General James Taylor.

Miliquist pulled a large pistol from his tote bag and loaded six shells. Again, he faced down range while he explained, "This weapon is a double action, Smith & Wesson ACP 45. The trigger both cocks the hammer and releases the hammer, which frees up my left index finger to become a *vertical sight* gauge,"

QUANTUM ROOTS II

Six more shots hit all six bulls-eyes.

Continued Miliquist, "I hope you also notice there's no real speed change throughout my draw. Just one smooth motion from start to finished. A top gun is never herky jerky.

"I must admit this is remarkable," said James Taylor, "And all from the hip. So, just how many gun enthusiasts can shoot like this?"

Bernie Miliquist packed up his tote bag and went on to explain that gun clubs like CAS and SASS have bred some top notch marksmen. Said Miliquist, "CAS stands for Cowboy Action Shooting, and SASS is the Single Action Shooting Society. Both clubs require you to shoot against the clock and fire weapons reminiscent of early America."

"I had no idea this movement existed," said the five star general, "This must have started when I was overseas."

The renewed interest in hand guns began on the West Coast in the 1980's, then gradually spread across the nation. Hollywood type stages were built for these would-be cowboys. Back drops depicted scenes from yesteryear. Props require the marksman to stop a bank robbery, draw against a cardboard silhouette, save a fair maiden, etc. Cash prizes are rare, ribbons plentiful. But, contestants do train to become a crack shot.

"And crack shots can become expert with the *point and shoot* technique," said Bernie Miliquist. "All it takes is practice and more practice and more practice, and real dedication."

"How many of these crack shots would use a large frame weapon like a forty-five?" asked the five star general noting that Miliquist favored a twenty-two or a light weight BB gun, "The military is no place for tinker toy weapons. When our targets go down, they stay down."

"Anybody who grips the gun with both hands can point and shoot with a large frame gun," explained Bernie, "I use light weapons because I shoot with one hand. My index finger points at the target, my middle finger pulls the trigger. Your security tapes show that the vigilante holds the gun with two hands. One index finger sights the target. The other index finger pulls the trigger."

"And he's not really fanning the weapon?" said agent Jeremy Wade.

"He's not fanning the weapon," replied Bernie Miliquist.

"So we're not necessarily looking for someone with giant hands and burly forearms," said Alexis for verification.

"I'm afraid your vigilante could be just about anybody," confirmed the special arms instructor, "Any gun enthusiast can learn *Point And Shoot.*"

"I'm not concerned about anybody," said James Taylor, "I'm concerned about this gunfighter who calls himself Leroy McCoy. I have a memo on my desk that says this man might have come through some kind of a wormhole."

"We have a coin" said Alexis, "The bartender at Nickles found a silver dollar on the floor, sometime after the shooting."

"Is the coin authentic?" boomed Taylor.

"Almost solid silver," said Alexis, "The front side shows Liberty sitting down. An eagle etches the back. The coin is dated 1870, and that date matches archive data we have from that era. Area newspaper articles mention a Leroy McCoy who rode herd as deputy marshal of Dodge City in 1876, shortly before Earp arrived."

"Wyatt Earp?"

"The same," chimed in Jeremy, "We deduced that if McCoy came through a wormhole from that era, this silver dollar might have come through the hole with McCoy."

KYLE KEYES

General James Taylor stared at Lieutenant General Alexis Grumman. His bushy eyebrows raised like two question marks as he asked, "And what's your take on this, Alexis ?"

"Jim, I don't believe in worm holes," said the lady general, "But, I was in the club when the gun fight occurred. This vigilante did look like a figure from yesteryear, and that fact puzzles me."

"Leroy McCoy did not come through a worm hole," said Bernie Miliquist.

"You seem very sure of yourself," said Alexis.

"I am."

"And what makes you so sure?" asked Alexis.

"Can we go to the projector room?" requested Bernie Miliquist.

"Of Course," replied the two generals as one voice.

A computer timer had locked the rear doors to the F.I.C. Building. Alexis' key card failed to work. Thus, the trio trudged over tar and cement to the front parking lot. They reunited with General James Ironhorse Taylor inside the revolving door. Asked Alexis, "Your screening room or mine?"

"Mine," boomed Taylor, "Peggy makes the better cup of coffee."

QUANTUM ROOTS II

Taylor's screen room was the second of two large rooms which constituted headquarters for the F.I.C. (Federal Intelligence Center.) The outer room housed lounge chairs, a receptionist and a coffee pot for impatient guests, foreign and stateside. The inner room held a conference table, numerous computers and one wall size viewing screen. The receptionist had stepped out, but the coffee was hot.

"Doug, bring up the film we have from Nickles security camera," said Alexis.

"Which clip?" asked the invisible techie from a hidden control room that fed the entire building.

"Which clip?" Alexis asked of Miliquist,

"We need a close up of the vigilante," answered Bernie Miliquist.

Focus was fuzzy and film jumpy, but eventually a life size picture of shooter and weapon filled the large wall screen. The vigilante looked indeed to be a figure from yesteryear. His trench coat featured giant lapels. His mustache curled up at the ends and looked too big for his weathered face. His leather boots were missing one spur. Said Bernie, "We need the draw."

"His draw is too fast for film," said the distant voice.

"Then show the shootings," replied Miliquist.

KYLE KEYES

The vigilante was right handed, as previously reported. He held a large frame 45 in two hands. His right index finger pulled the trigger. His left index finger pointed toward the target.

"I rest my case," said Bernie Miliquist.

"You've lost me," replied Alexis Grumman.

"He's using the *point and shoot* method for firing a handgun," said Miliquist, "This part of the clip has been all over the news. This is the technique I just demonstrated out on the gun range. I guess the rest of the clip was too graphic to show on television, but it was this portion that caught my attention."

"And this news clip told you that the vigilante didn't come through a wormhole?" inquired Alexis.

"No ma'am," replied Bernie, "The morning news hounds told me that. Newspaper records verified that one Samuel Leroy McCoy died in May of 1887. Those records claimed that Marshal McCoy was shot in the back in the small town of Deadwood."

"He was," confirmed Alexis Grumman.

"But the double action revolver didn't come out until 1889, and the *point and shoot* technique you just saw on this film clip, requires a double action revolver."

"I see," said General Taylor breaking into the two way conversation, "So what's the bottom line here, soldier?"

Concluded Miliquist who was a civilian and not a soldier,, "Frankly sir, it's not likely that the real Leroy McCoy ever fired anything but a single action peace maker. That's the nick name the Army gave the Colt 45."

"Which means this Marshall Leroy McCoy is not the real McCoy," said Taylor, thoughtfully, "If you will pardon the pun."

"So pardoned," replied Bernie Miliquist.

"So pardoned," echoed Alexis Grumman, "And so much for worm holes."

*   *   *   *   *

Despite Miliquist's case against a possible worm hole, General James Taylor elected to keep all *Vigilante Sightings* with Alexis Grumman and the Department for Paranormal Activities. Taylor based his decision on the lack of evidence that Olan Chapman and Samuel Leroy McCoy were the same person. Taylor acknowledged the similarities between the White Plains sighting and the current shooting, but pointed out that the playhouse vigilante and the local pub vigilante may not have been the same vigilante.

Chapter 8

Nickles reopened to soon find Alexis Grumman and Jeremy Ward back at the window booth with the small heart carved into the tabletop. Blood stains were gone from the hardwood floor, as was Frankie the bouncer. Tony the bar tender still worked the dinner shift.

"Where's Molly?" asked Jeremy.

"Out with a fever," replied Tony grabbing an order pad, "Anything on this vigilante?"

"Nada," said Alexis, "I'll have ribs and rice."

"Make that two," said Jeremy..

"Stanley was in earlier," said Tony still fishing, "Stanley claims this guy could be anybody."

"Stanley our door guard?" asked Alexis.

"The same," said Tony, "Stanley says the worm hole theory has been tossed out."

"We'll take the beer first," said Alexis.

"Coming right up," said Tony, "Anyway, I said to Stanley that this guy can't be just anybody, because not just anybody can shoot like that."

QUANTUM ROOTS II

"Tony, this is agency business," said Alexis, "I'll speak to Stanley when I get back to work."

"Yes ma'am."

The D. P. A. had the fingerprint report back from New York State. The prints taken from the White Plains playhouse piano belonged to Olan Chapman. Thus, authorities knew for certain that the slender computer geek had survived the bullet riddled, boat ride over Niagara Falls, which meant his alter ego, Jesse Joe Jacks still lived. Unfortunately, forensic experts could not use fingerprints to tie a Leroy McCoy to either man.

"Understandable," said Jeremy, "McCoy would never have been fingerprinted."

"Exactly," replied Alexis.

"But why do we care," said Jeremy, "I thought you were satisfied that Marshall McCoy did not come through a wormhole."

"True," agreed Alexis, "However, we cannot be sure that Olan Chapman is not a reincarnation of Leroy McCoy."

"Really?"

"Really."

"Alexis, you're beginning to sound like Norman Daly," said the junior agent, referring to the author who wrote the book entitled *Quantum Roots,* that derailed standard universe theories.

"God forbid that I sound like rocket science," said Alexis, "However, mounting evidence continues to suggest that people do form from recycled energy."

"So what do we have here?" asked Jeremy.

"You have been eyeball to eyeball with Leroy McCoy and Jesse Joe Jacks ," said Alexis munching on a spinach salad, "Why don't you weigh in here."

"Do I get to go on top?"

"Let's talk about Jesse Joe Jacks," said Alexis.

Jeremy Wade's confrontation with Jesse Joe Jacks occurred in the dead of winter, when the junior agent tracked the armed fugitive to an eerie cabin deep in the South Jersey Pinelands. Fresh snow covered the ground. Icy winds cut through tree tops. The Pinelands can be scary enough without moving shadows, and shotgun blasts echoing in the distance. This infamous wasteland is rich in folkways and folklore. City dwellers who leave the main road for a shortcut to the ocean, often vanish in these gloomy woods. Much of the 3.1 million acres is uninhabited. If you stay lost long enough, the countless sandy trails that lead nowhere begin to dig tiny graves in the mind. On this particular day, the trackee got behind the tracker, and scared Jeremy out his jockey shorts.

QUANTUM ROOTS II

"I was not wearing underwear."

"Yes Jeremy," said Alexis, "We know that."

Agent Wade was halfway through the Miranda Rights when Jesse Joe Jacks drew and fired two rounds. Each shot nipped a draw string on Jeremy's snow suit. The trousers fell first. Then, Jeremy's video recorder landed between his feet, camera lens pointed up.

"Every secretary in the building had an eye on a screen monitor that day," recalled Alexis, "Even Amy."

"You mean the Amy who was once an Amos?"

"The same. . and Jeremy. . .if that weapon goes off in here, you will be back on unpaid leave."

"I intend to be ready for my next encounter with trouble," said Jeremy fumbling around with his service revolver, "Whoever that trouble might be."

"Jeremy, stick with your pepper spray."

"What if I'm downwind?"

"How about Judo?"

"I have weak wrists."

Bartender Tony set up the second round of beers that wrapped up happy hour and wiped off the booth table. He disappeared into the kitchen with the empty mugs when Alexis said, "Let's take the silver dollar out of the equation, and forget the fact that one man is right handed and the other left."

"Ignore the rare coin we found ?"

"Negate the silver dollar."

The junior agent holstered his service revolver. He sipped foam from the frosty beer mug. He stared blankly ahead and said, "I think they are the same man, Alexis."

"Who's the same man?"

"Olan Chapman, Jesse Joe Jacks and this Leroy McCoy are all the same person."

"Based on what?" asked Alexis.

"The lip mole," explained Jeremy pointing to a spot on his own mouth, "All three men have the same lip mole right here."

"I see," said the DPA director, "You're sure of this?"

"I know what I saw," said Jeremy, "It's hard to spot it on this latest film, but it's there."

"So in that case," said Alexis, "We're looking for Olan Chapman and his alter ego, by any name."

"Yes," agreed Jeremy.

Said a thoughtful Alexis Grumman, "Multiple personalities would be an answer, and if so, that would explain the *point and shoot* technique. McCoy may not have mastered *point and shoot*, but we know that Jacks was a crack shot using that method."

QUANTUM ROOTS II

"So, we are back to a worm hole."

"A mental worm hole," conceded Alexis.

"But, that does not explain the clothes and the gun," said Jeremy, "Also, Olan Chapman and Jesse Joe Jacks are left handed. Yet, this new gunfighter is right-handed."

Alexis finished eating and opened her classified communicator. Although she was the senior agent here, she did value her companion's input when he was not in his clownish mode. She clicked on *memo notes* as she said, "I've been doing some homework on this left-hand-right hand issue. I called the Hobbs Creek Police Station and talked to an Isabel Jackson who put me in touch with former Police Chief, Adam Quayle."

"Chief Quayle and I worked together on the Pandarus File case," said Jeremy suddenly sitting up, "Some called it the murder mystery of the century. I'm not sure if that's true, but it did take forty odd years to solve, along with a stroke of providence."

The Pandarus File documented the gruesome kill of an autism boy at a shooting range in Hobbs Creek, New Jersey. The case went unsolved from 1958 to post 911, when the principle suspect turned up accidentally in the Right Bank section of Paris, France. It was young Jeremy Wade's first overseas assignment. His stateside contacts were Adam Quayle and Jeeter Potts.

"I wanted to track down this Jeeter Potts," said the lady general, "Our data banks show that Sergeant Jeeter Potts and Olan Chapman were one time pinocle partners."

"Desk Sergeant Potts worked for Quayle," said Jeremy, "What prompted you to call Potts?"

"Just playing a hunch," said Alexis, "I wanted to see what Potts could tell me about Chapman."

"Did Quayle put you in touch with Potts?"

"He did," said Alexis.

"And ?"

"Potts told me that Chapman dealt cards left handed. ..and . right handed. Potts claims that Chapman had such finger dexterity, he could deal cards with just one hand."

"Ambidextrous," murmured Jeremy.

Alexis signed for the meal, waited for Tony to move on, and then said to Jeremy, "I have to believe if Chapman can handle a deck of cards with either hand, he can handle a gun with either hand."

"Point taken," said Jeremy.

"However," continued Alexis, "That does not explain how the vigilante happened to show up here, and why."

QUANTUM ROOTS II

Jeremy finished his beer and stared out the pub window at a blue funnel, formed by tree foliage that opened to the sky. Said the junior agent, "It has to be a worm hole. . . .Chapman pops in and out of some kind of time warp."

"Jeremy, I can't accept time warp."

"But, our brain and our galaxy have a common denominator," said Jeremy, "They both consist of 90% dark matter. So, maybe your *mental worm hole* is the answer. Maybe it's a mental time warp. Maybe it's Chapman's brain that goes through some kind of metamorphose."

"Maybe," said Alexis.

"Maybe he's looking for you."

"Jeremy, we've been over this ground... .the vigilante would not be looking for me."

"No, but Olan Chapman might be."

"You're suggesting a cat and mouse game?"

"That has to be considered," replied Jeremy.

"So. . .maybe it's time we revisit Dr Norman Daly for an update on his book, Quantum Roots," said Alexis inching out of the booth, "And what made you ask about that waitress?"

"Molly?"

"Yes, Molly."

KYLE KEYES

"I'd like to talk about General Taylor," said the junior agent fishing for a table tip.

"Do I sense a bit of jealousy here?"

"My eyes aren't green," countered Jeremy.

"Truce," said Alexis waving a white table napkin, "Your shower or mine?"

"Mine."

"I hope you got the hot water fixed."

"I have some new wine, a Cabernet."

"You didn't get the water heater fixed."

"I think you'll like it."

"I think we'll go to my place."

Chapter 9

The jumbo jet dropped through blowing rain and bounced onto the Nassau International runway. Once inside the Lynden Pindling terminal, Jeremy Wade sought the rendezvous sign that read Baggage Weight Allowances. Soon, two men dressed in Hawaiian shirts and black knee socks, pushed their way through the maze of hugs, kisses and rolling suitcases.

"As I recall, it rained last time I flew in here," said the special agent pumping hands with Dr. Norman Arnold Daly. "I must remember to bring a raincoat next time."

"Welcome back to the tropics," said the noted author and retired physicist. Then, nodding toward the third man, Daly said, "Jeremy, this is Dr Harold Lee Daly, author of the best seller *Two Minds One Body*. Maybe you have read it?"

"I need to catch up on my reading," confessed the special agent, "Are you two brothers?"

"Twins," replied Harold Daly, "I'm the good looking one. Norman here is the evil one."

Jeremy, does that man have a black mustache and an orange goatee?

Both men have a black mustache and an orange goatee, text ed back the special agent.

I'm having second thoughts about this meeting, replied Alexis Grumman, who made the flight plans for Jeremy to revisit this world renowned physicist, now retired and writing books. *Keep it short and get back here.*

"Hungry?"   asked Norman Daly.

"Always,"   said Jeremy,   "Is that fish place still in business?"

The three men drove through busy downtown Nassau and parked in the sandy lot of the popular fish fry. They climbed a rickety, wooden staircase and found an empty table on the upper deck. Dr Norman Arnold Daly ordered a customary whiskey on the rocks. Jeremy opted for soda, while Harold Daly declined beverage.

"You are not thirsty ?"   asked a dark skinned waiter with fat lips and a white apron.

"I am very thirsty,"   said Harold Daly looking over the drink menu.

"Is there a problem, monsieur?"

"I do not see a listing for Cosmopolitan,"   said Harold Daly.

QUANTUM ROOTS II

"We don't stock cranberry juice," replied the waiter, "Does monsieur have a second choice?"

"Maybe a Cape Codder?"

"I can bring you the vodka," said the waiter.

"I'll take water."

"Yes, monsieur,"

"The commonwealth does not know this," said Harold Daly, "But cranberry juice can help ward off urinary tract infections."

"I didn't know that myself," replied Jeremy.

Jeremy, we are not here to talk about cranberry juice and urinary infections. We need Dr Harold Daly's input on Multiple Personality Disorder.

"Ten four."

"And, we need to revisit Norman Daly's book, Quantum Roots."

"Will do." replied the junior agent.

Sudden wind gusts lifted a table umbrella and blew the yellow shade cover over the deck railing and into some distant picnic benches. The three men took nature's hint and quickly found a table inside. Harold Daly opened his book, *Two Minds One Body.* He then opened a manila folder faxed from F.I.C. headquarters in Warrenton, Va, and paused to stare over reading glasses at Jeremy Wade. Asked the noted psychiatrist,

KYLE KEYES

"This Lieutenant General Grumman is your boss ?"

"She is," replied the special agent.

"She seems very blunt."

"She has great legs," said Jeremy.

Harold Daly coughed up an ice cube and traced a review finger over the first pages. The data covered the vigilante shootings, fingerprint reports and Olan Chapman's suicide attempt at Niagara Falls. Questions asked, pertained to Multiple Personality Disorder, and the underlying cause for character transformation from Olan Chapman to the vigilante, and visa versus.

"Trauma is most times the key," explained the noted psychiatrist, "Chapman's bout with Dissociative Identity Disorder (DID) most likely started, when he witnessed three older boys rape and murder his older sister. Such traumatic events often lead to memory impairment. The ugly deed gets buried in the subconscious, and then resurfaces sometime later. I believe this is the case with Olan Chapman"

Continued Harold Daly, "This dossier outlines a car accident Chapman had two years back. He suffered a head concussion which led to a coma. I can't be sure, but it's possible that the coma opened the door to a previous ego."

QUANTUM ROOTS II

"Damn," exclaimed Jeremy Wade, "Sounds like science fiction."

"All is not as it sounds," said Harold Daly.

"That calls for another whiskey on the rocks," said Norman Daly.

Jeremy, what causes these transformations?

"Dr Daly, what causes the personality change between Olan Chapman and his alter ego?" asked Jeremy relaying the text message from F.I.C.

"Nitric Oxide," replied Harold Day.

What !!!

Harold Daly paused to finish brunch. He wiped yellow egg yolk from his orange goatee, and dropped a second ice cube into his coffee. He watched a busty waitress lean over an adjoining table as he said, "Olan Chapman probably has a high level of Nitric Oxide in his body chemistry. Nitric Oxide raises testosterone levels, which in turn cause a blood rush. Men use this technique for penis enlargement."

Jeremy, listen to this carefully.

You are not funny, Alexis.

I don't want to step on your male ego, Jeremy. But, you can't jump either.

"Nitric Oxide is not a substance," continued Harold Daly, "Nitric Oxide is a gas caused by certain dietary foods, and you will get a chuckle out of this- two of those foods are oats and lettuce."

"Damn," said Jeremy Wade, "You think Olan Chapman's running around eating rabbit food?"

"I doubt it," replied Harold Daly, "But he could be taking the blue pill."

I hope you are taking notes, Jeremy.

Alexis, I don't need the blue pill !

Harold Daly went on to suggest that any trauma in Olan Chapman's life, might kick off a blood rush that would change the computer geek into the vigilante. Daly said the metamorphosis could last up to four hours. After which, the vigilante would revert back to Olan Chapman. Concluded Daly, "I'm sure I have peers who will disagree. Jekyll and Hyde arguments range from *maybe* to *absurd*. However, I believe this Olan Chapman is the real deal. In summary, he possesses the real alter ego. As Chapman, Olan's brain cells draw from his own experiences. As the vigilante, Chapman has a separate autobiographical memory that appears to come from a former life, as opposed to all experiences coming from this life. He may or may not have some control over dissociation (DID). He may or may not have a common sense of self. Truthfully, I would give up my baseball card collection to be his therapist."

QUANTUM ROOTS II

Jeremy, move the conversation onto wormholes and you better not be drinking a beer. I need a current opinion on wormholes.

Harold Daly smiled while replying, "Norman's in charge of sci-fi and paranormal events. I try to stay this side of the Twilight Zone."

Unperturbed, brother Norman opened a copy of his controversial book *Quantum Roots*, and pointed to an illustration that resembled a giant turbine. Said the retired physicist, "This is a picture of the LHC. (Large Hadron Collider). Man-made fury you might say. Recently, this energy collider has verified what nineteenth century experiments could only suggest."

"Such as?" queried Jeremy Wade.

"Energy bits do have a quantum state as well as a particle state. Every bit of matter has a corresponding fleck of ant-matter. Also, bosons and fermions have different quantum characteristics. Any number of force particles can occupy quantum space, but only one quark can occupy it's own quantum state."

"Meaning?" asked Jeremy Wade.

"Quarks will retain basic properties regardless of time and space," bubbled Dr. Norman Daly, "And it's the quarks that define the object. This could open the door to real interplanetary travel."

I hope he's not suggesting that Chapman and McCoy are leaping through time and space.

"I hope you don't mean that Olan Chapman and Marshal Leroy McCoy are leaping through time and space," relayed Jeremy Wade.

"This is not TV," smiled Dr Norman Daly, "This is nature's quantum leap. We all have our own genetic code. We all have our own fingerprints. And while we appear to come from our parents, we actually come through our parents."

Therefore, two different couples could produce the same DNA?

"That's not likely in a given cycle of a given star system," replied Norman Daly, "Current revelations do suggest that creation forms from recycled energy. However, it needs to be noted that the odds of two different couples, producing the same genetic code in a given galaxy, would be like catching lightning in a bottle. For starters, current human gene count is twenty thousand plus. Now, add in the 3.1 million energy bits that format with each gene, and you get the really big picture."

"How about other galaxies?" asked Jeremy.

"Space/Time has no limit," replied Dr. Norman Daly, "There could be a star system for every grain of sand. However, it's also not likely that your vigilante would show up in another galaxy. It's more conceivable that he would have been born in a previous cycle of the Milky Way."

"The Milky Way has been here, before?" text ed in Alexis Grumman.

"Of course," said Norman Daly responding to Jeremy Wade's relay of the question, "That's what my book Quantum Roots is about. Quarks define creation, and quarks retain their properties going in and coming out of black holes. Bare in mind, all galaxies contain a black hole. However, it doesn't matter if galaxies show up individually or in a group. Eventually, a given galaxy can spawn a life form that has developed in a previous cycle of that galaxy."

Can or will ?

"Can," replied Norman Daly, "We can't verify that it will."

"But we do have an 1887 record of a Marshal Samuel Leroy McCoy who was ambushed in Deadwood, South Dakota," said Jeremy Wade relaying a text from Alexis Grumman.

"Which means this McCoy and his family tree showed up in this cycle of the Milky Way," explained Norman Daly, "All they required was livable conditions and the order of natural selection. "

Jeremy, ask Doctor Daly if our Olan Chapman could be this Marshal Samuel Leroy McCoy?

"Only if he beat those incredible odds," replied Norman Daly to the text message,, "And that's not likely. It's more conceivable that Olan Chapman had a previous life as a gunfighter, in a previous life cycle. He may have picked up the name Leroy McCoy from reading material."

Jeremy, put me on the speaker phone.

Roger that..

"Dr Daly?" said Alexis cutting in vocally.

"Yes ma'am?"

"I'm Lt General Grumman."

"Yes ma'am."

"I'm director for the department of paranormal activities," said Alexis, "I believe that scientists have recently identified 355 genes that kicked off life on this planet some four billion years ago, plus or minus."

"More evolutionary nonsense !" cried Norman Daly, "These scientists are blind dogs chasing their own tail. It needs to be noted that creation is beyond comprehension, but creation is not magic. Evolution on the other hand is illusion. If our birth depended on evolution, we would never beat the odds to get here.

QUANTUM ROOTS II

Which brings us back to my book, *Quantum Roots*, which states that people form from recycled energy. Trust me, your elusive vigilante shows up because he's in the deck when the trick starts."

"Doctor, do you believe in worm holes?" asked the director for paranormal events.

"Creation is a worm hole," replied Norman Daly, "Atoms require hadrons to form a nucleus, and each hadron comes through it's own worm hole. Two quarks form the bi-dimensional plane needed to support the hole. The remaining quark – with or without an electron - squeezes through this hole. After which, the first two quarks follow, shaping the hadron to fit into a given genetic, configuration. The hole then closes to divide time from timeless."

Jeremy, what happened to our video?

I'm making notes.

I think you're taking pictures of that girl at the bar, text ed Alexis.

The brown waiter with fat lips and white apron sat a cold beer on the canvas table cover. A gold tooth flashed as he pushed the drink toward Jeremy and said, "Compliments from the mademoiselle at the bar."

Jeremy, are you drinking a beer?

I'm eating lobster and corn fritters, Alexis.

I think you are drinking a beer, Jeremy.

"Your wife?" inquired Harold Daly sneaking a peek at the agent's classified communicator.

"My boss," replied Jeremy.

"She was just on the phone with us?"

"Yes," replied Jeremy.

"The one with the great legs?"

"She likes it on top," said Jeremy.

"Bravo," grinned Harold Daly.

Jeremy, I need a third opinion before we waste anymore agency money on this assignment. You are on your way to Buffalo for a meeting with Dr. Adler Dearwood.

Are we both going, boss?

No, you are going, solo.

I think you are jealous over the girl at the bar, text ed Jeremy.

I'm not jealous.

Alexis, I think you're jealous.

I'm not jealous and forgive the blue pill slur.

Forgiven, text ed Jeremy.

You are not old enough for the blue pill.

"I take it this interview is finished," said the retired physicist.

"A cab is coming to pick me up," said Jeremy.

QUANTUM ROOTS II

"Agent Wade," said Harold Daly after Norman Daly left in search of a bathroom, "My brother was asked to leave the science institute sometime back, and take his book with him – along with his thousand notes on bosons, quarks, photons, fermions, leptons, etc, etc, etc."

"I see," said Jeremy Wade setting down a beer mug, "So, his views are not necessarily your views?"

"He's my brother," said Harold Daly staring at Norman's empty whiskey glass, "As the song goes, *He Ain't Heavy.* Any other questions?"

"Yes."

"Ask."

"It's personal," said Jeremy.

"So ask."

"My girlfriend is old enough to be my mother," explained Jeremy Wade turning off his cell phone while hedging a glance at the renowned psychiatrist.

"And?"

"I could be just a replacement for her son," said Jeremy, "As a teenager, she bore a boy out of wedlock. The father vanished before she left maternity, and now the son fails to keep up communication."

Alexis Grumman's father was stationed at Fort Benning, Ga. when the teenage Alexis became pregnant by a corporal platooned on Sand Hill. Desert Storm was just heating up. By the time Alexis left Martin Army Hospital, the baby's father was AWOL somewhere in Canada. Grabbing boot straps and sucking it up, Alexis began her own officer training right there on Main Post. Over the next two decades, she toted Skip Jr on a military career that would encompass the globe.

"Skip Jr?" smiled Harold Daly.

"He was named after his father," said Jeremy, "He would be my age by now . . the son I mean."

"Jeremy, if this Alexis pops your cork, then she's the one for you."

"Really?"

"Enjoy the wine."

"Really?"

"Really.

"What do I owe you?" bubbled Jeremy Wade.

"Just leave the tip," said a smiling Harold Daly as a taxi horn sounded, downstairs.

Chapter 10

The name on the curbside mailbox read D A. Dearwood. The D A. stood for Doctor Adler, with the *r* missing after the initial *D*, because doctors no longer promote house calls. The house was a valid stone mansion squeezed between single story cottages that matched the rest of this Buffalo City suburb. The lawns looked like green strips pasted on a terrain of tar and cement.

Adler Dearwood originally planned to sell this estate upon retirement and move to the country. Then, wife Helen came down with Alzheimer, and ivy covered, cottage dreams faded as Helen deteriorated. Today would have been Adler and Helen's golden wedding anniversary.

"I can come back on a better day," said Jeremy Wade while being led to a sitting room that overlooked a pool, "I did not know."

"Every day is pretty much the same now," said Dr Dearwood, "You wanted to talk to me about Olan Chapman?"

KYLE KEYES

"Yes, Olan Chapman had a previous life as game warden Jesse Joe Jacks," said Jeremy, "We can prove that with fingerprints. But, we can't prove that Chapman and Leroy McCoy are the same person. All we have is circumstantial evidence."

"Leroy McCoy?" queried Dearwood.

"Our new vigilante," replied Jeremy.

"Of course, it's been in the headlines," said the former Buffalo City psychiatrist, "How can I help you?"

Talk about Chapman's childhood, text ed Alexis.

"Tell me about the young Olan Chapman," said Jeremy.

"I just made fresh coffee," offered Dearwood.

"I would love a cup," said Jeremy.

Olan Ford Chapman was born to a William and Hildegard Chapman in Buffalo, NY on August 8 1974. The boy grew up behind locked gates, and attended a private school. When he turned eight years old, he watched three high school boys rape and murder his older sister who attended a public school. Young Olan ran and hid. Two years later, the family relocated to the Hyde Park area of Niagara Falls. A prominent therapist prescribed the move to help young Olan forget the horrific event.

QUANTUM ROOTS II

"I was that therapist," said Dearwood rubbing tired eyes. He ran wrinkled fingers through thinning hair and went on to explain, "I tried to convince young Olan that his instinct for survival probably saved his life. However, the nightmares carried more weight than my counseling. Painfully, he grew up regarding himself as a coward."

"Sometimes, retreat is the better part of valor," agreed Jeremy reading the medical diplomas that hung over a brown leather sofa. He tested the coffee and said, "I took a psychology course back in college."

Jeremy, text ed Alexis, *You are dropping sugar cubes on the floor.*

"Your boss?" asked Adler Dearwood peering at Jeremy's two-way video phone.

"My boss."

"She watches you closely."

"She bitches a lot."

Jeremy !!!

A white poodle chased a black cat from the pool area, through the kitchen and into the sitting room. The dog stopped to lick the sugar cubes off the varnished floor.

"The dog's name is Whitey," said Dearwood petting the tiny poodle, "The cat's name is Blackie."

"Well, there's no mistaking which is which," said Jeremy.

Jeremy, ask Dearwood about DID

"Dissociative Identity Disorder," answered Adler Dearwood as Jeremy switched his phone to speaker mode, "Previously known as MPD, Multiple Personality Disorder, identified by more than one behavior pattern surfacing from the same individual. Symptoms include memory lapses, total amnesia, headaches, anxiety and alcohol abuse. All of these symptoms characterize Olan Chapman, of course."

"Seems we are on the same page, doctor" said Alexis now talking via Jeremy's speaker phone, "Just what causes this personality change to take place?"

"Emotion can be the trigger," said Dearwood, echoing the possible explanation given by Harold Daly, "Persons with DID usually suffer from guilt, fear, or some form of childhood trauma. Then, some current event takes place, and emotion pulls the trigger. And here again we are talking about Olan Chapman."

"My data bank shows that Chapman once led a march to ban handguns," said Alexis.

"Right through downtown Buffalo," verified Dr Dearwood, "I still practiced at the time. Gail -that was my nurse – called me to the window, and there was

Olan leading this small parade of flag wavers. Slogans were varied, but they all called for a gun ban."

"So why would Olan become a gunfighter?" asked Alexis.

"I'll get to that in a minute," replied Dearwood pausing to fix more coffee. He accepted a decline from Jeremy and then with a faint smile, offered Alexis a cup over the phone line.

"Maybe you could send me a cup through a worm hole," challenged Alexis, baiting a hook.

"Do you believe in worm holes?" asked the good doctor.

"Only in apples."

"Touche," said Adler Dearwood.

"Are you familiar with a Dr Norman Arnold Daly?" asked Alexis.

"The Quantum Roots physicist?"

"The same," replied Alexis, "Daly believes we form from recycled energy. Daly believes that we are what we were, and we are what we're going to be."

"I met Dr Daly in Nassau and what an honor that was," said Jeremy.

"Then he must have filled you in on Quarks, Bosons, Fermions, time and space relativity," said the noted psychiatrist sitting up straighter in a swivel chair missing a leg castor, "I would give up a gold filling to have been there. You must have left with a deeper insight of the man and his mission?"

"He drinks a lot," said Jeremy.

"Did he explain his findings on how quarks and their properties relate to a black hole?"

"I didn't catch all of that," said Jeremy.

"Jeremy was flirting with a cocktail waitress," said Alexis over the speaker phone.

Continued Dr Dearwood putting the subject matter back on track, "Daly bases his quantum root theory on two 21st Century discoveries: Quarks are energy bits that define our genetic road map; also, quarks retain their properties going into a black hole, and coming back out, to where they begin a fresh cycle, undamaged and unchanged. Consequently, Daly suggests that we cannot have true definition without repetition, which is the foundation for his reincarnation views."

"You really are a Dr Daly fan," noted Alexis.

"I've read all his books," replied Dearwood.

"Interesting," said Alexis via the squeaky phone speaker, "A doctor studying a physicist. Now, can you tell me about your views as a certified doctor and noted psychologist."

QUANTUM ROOTS II

"Psychiatrist," corrected Adler Dearwood, "A psychologist studies mental disorders, a psychiatrist both studies and treats mental disorders."

"I stand corrected," said Alexis popping a mint and taking a cold water drink in front of the wall screen back at headquarters.

"That's okay," said Dearwood through a weak smile, "People get the two mixed up all the time. So, let us suppose that Norman Daly is right. Perhaps we don't go around once, but live an endless chain of lives. In that case, it becomes very conceivable that Olan Chapman could have been a gunfighter. ..and.. .on more than one occasion,

"Now we bring another fact into the equation," continued Dearwood, "Many Gunfighters of yore were men of small statue. Handguns and quick draws were their equalizer. Many of these gunfighters suffered from what we now call, *The Little Man Syndrome*."

"And Olan Chapman is a man small in statue," said Alexis Grumman.

"He is," replied Dearwood.

"But Chapman hates guns," said Alexis for a second time.

"And that's the piece that fills in the puzzle," explained Adler Dearwood, "Nature gives every living specimen some type of armor. A turtle gets a shell. A rabbit is fleet of foot. An endangered bird can fly away, and so on and so on. Olan Chapman hates guns. But there are times when the gun becomes his only tool for survival. Thus, his subconscious turns back the sands of time. He becomes a person he used to be. A person who doesn't hate the gun, and knows how to use one."

"But he's suicidal," said Alexis.

"He appears to be suicidal," corrected Adler Dearwood, "He needs to convince the world that he's not afraid to die."

"Or convince himself?" queried Alexis.

"Correct."

"Fascinating," said Alexis, "But why would today's Olan Chapman hate guns if he once lived by the gun."

"Who knows," replied Dearwood, "Maybe he's destined to die by the gun. We are all trapped in a circumstance of our own making."

"You have given this case a lot of thought," said Alexis.

"A busy mind sidetracks depression," said the recent widower. Then at visit's end, Adler and Jeremy Wade passed a hallway photo of Helen Dearwood that brought talk back to Alzheimer. Dearwood was with his

QUANTUM ROOTS II

wife on the morning she passed away. Her brain literally disconnected from the body. Her legs kicked, arms shook. One eye rolled around and around and around and around. Three hours later, she died. The two men shook hands at the front door where Dearwood said,

"Good luck catching Olan Chapman."

"I'm sorry for your loss," said Jeremy.

Eventually, things got better for Adler Dearwood. They just never got good again.

Chapter 11

Alexis snapped off her classified communicator to break connection with Adler Dearwood. She moved away from the giant wall screen, with the video two-way in the lower corner. She paused to inspect her own image in a side mirror. Her hair needed a fresh dye job, her oval face couldn't cut it anymore without makeup. A sagging jaw line and age spots were now the enemy, as was raw daylight. Her right foot suffered from a gout flare-up. Her back hurt from a long night with Jeremy before he left for Buffalo. She muttered something inaudible and then said out loud, "Doug would you date a girl half your age?"

"I would love to," said the invisible technician behind the wall screen, "Do you want any Canadian cities on your map?"

"No, just show the states."

"Roger that."

Justice might stall occasionally, but technology moves on. Alexis grabbed a computer wand and began outlining the zig-zag route taken by the vigilante. As she tapped each city on the big board, a birds-eye circle would appear. Two taps would convert the inset to 3-D. A prolonged tap would trigger a closeup.

"What happened to push pins and chalk?" said Alexis with a faint smile.

"I don't know," said the invisible techie, "That was before my time."

"You're full of bullshit, Doug," said Alexis staring at Western New York State. Then she asked, "I can understand why the Vigilante showed up in Buffalo City, because that was Chapman's old stomping grounds. But, if he wanted to come here, why did he go east to Salem, New Hampshire?"

"Who knows," said the invisible technician, "Maybe he was lost or confused or intoxicated."

"Intoxicated?" mused Alexis, "Drunk ..yes, that's a possibility. . .or maybe confused. . .but not lost. Olan Chapman is never lost. The man has a computer for a brain with a built in GPS."

"Do you think that his two identities know each other?" asked Doug resizing the aerial map to fit the screen.

"Dearwood can't be sure," replied Alexis, "And now we make the case fuzzier. Chapman goes from

KYLE KEYES

Salem, New Hampshire to Danbury, Connecticut, and on to White Plains, New York, all on the East Coast. Then, he travels west to reach our pub here in Virginia. We are overlooking something. I can feel it. These cities must have a common denominator."

"Maybe he's looking for you," said Doug.

"That's what Jeremy thinks," replied Alexis.

"Just don't be standing next to me," said Doug, "I have a lot of children to feed."

Alexis couldn't help but smile. Doug the invisible technician was Douglas Q Kramer, the Q for Quantity. Kramer fathered twenty children via three wives, and with health and college costs on the rise, everyone was counting. The hayride now over, wives *one* and *two* had Kramer by the wallet, while lawyers applied financial pressure. Alexis popped a candy mint and took a quick swallow of cold water. Grinning, she suggested that dating a younger girl was not an answer for the toothy technician. Then, she moved back to the wall screen and said, "Doug, run that security tape again."

"Which one?"

"The one from Nickles Bar."

"We have looked at that a dozen times," said the techie.

"One more time won't hurt," replied Alexis.

QUANTUM ROOTS II

Fate wears many faces, much like a winter snow-fall. Early, late, beautiful, sloppy. At this particular moment in time, fate chose to be helpful. Doug accidentally started the film at a point before Alexis and Jeremy entered the pub, and this fresh look brought the lady general to attention.

"What is it, boss?" asked Doug.

"Roll back the film," ordered Alexis.

"Roger."

"Stop !" ordered Alexis, "Check you monitor."

"Checking."

"Who are the two guys standing at the bar?"

"Can't be sure," said Doug, "Looks to be our two marines."

"And who's the guy standing between the two marines?"

"Sonofabitch!" replied the projectionist moving the film frame by frame for a better look, "It's Olan Chapman. . .Chapman was in the pub before you got there, and he looks to be arguing with those two marines who got out of hand."

"Chapman was at the pub !!" cried Alexis.

"We have no audio," said Doug.

"I can read lips," said Alexis, "Chapman just told that one marine to go fuck himself."

Frankie The Bouncer was nowhere in sight. The two marines dragged Olan Chapman down the rest room hallway and threw the slender computer wizard out the back door. The marines then returned to the bar as Alexis and Jeremy entered the front door. After which the brawl began that ended with the vigilante coming in the front door and killing the two marines.

"So maybe this Chapman really is gunning for you," said a now sober Douglas Q. Kramer.

"Olan Chapman would not be gunning for anybody," mused Alexis, "And his alter ego wouldn't know who I am. He could have shot me right there and then. Instead, he saved Jeremy . .no. . .your earlier thought was right. He was there to make contact."

"With you?"

"With me," replied Alexis.

"As Olan Chapman?"

"As Olan Chapman," confirmed Alexis.

"Why?" asked the invisible projectionist.

"Who knows," replied Alexis, who then moved to the big screen and had Doug re-run all the security film taken from Nickles Bar And Grille. The hallway camera showed the restroom doors and rear entrance.. The front door camera covered the window booths and dining room. But it was the bar camera that turned the trick. Chapman's stool was empty when the vigilante burst through the front door. Murmured Alexis, "So we finally got some hard proof. Olan Chapman is Samuel LeRoy McCoy."

"I wonder why forensics failed to come up with prints," asked the invisible technician.

"Look at the film," replied Alexis, "Chapman was wearing gloves."

KYLE KEYES

PART TWO

KYLE   KEYES

Chapter 12

Two weeks passed with no vigilante sightings. Jeremy Wade then got the following text message from DPA Director, Alexis Grumman.

Come in.

"I need to see some ID," said Stanley the door guard.

"Stanley, will you wipe off your glasses," whined Jeremy at the top step to the F.I.C. building, "It's me, Special Agent Jeremy Wade. I work here."

"I know you work here," said the silver haired senior, "Just doing my job. Nobody gets past this first checkpoint without proper ID."

"What's the eighteen wheeler doing in our park--ing lot?" asked Jeremy.

"That's Jeremiah Jackson," replied Stanley, "He runs a one man trucking business. He picked up the vigilante, hitchhiking,"

"Does Alexis know about this?"

"He's with her right now," said the frail door guard checking Jeremy's ID, "And have your credentials ready next time."

"Yes sir," said Jeremy.

"And you can scrap the phony salute," said the front door guard, "Some of us take our job, seriously."

Jeremy Wade reached the second check point in time to see an inner guard turn back two camel jockeys, a mass of tattooed arms waving *gay* signs, and a naked man in a raincoat. Said the second guard, "Some guy named Jeremiah Jackson picked up the vigilante, hitch--hiking. He's with your boss right now. You better get in there, pronto."

"If this isn't a breach of security," asked Jeremy Wade, "Just where did you get this information?"

"Stanley told me," said the inner guard, "There was more but I didn't catch all of it."

*   *   *   *   *

"This is Jeremiah Jackson," said Alexis as Jeremy entered the inner office of the DPA, "Jeremiah is a big rig driver who picked up the vigilante, hitchhiking."

"Who's hiring these security guards?" asked the junior agent.

"We're on a budget, Jeremy," replied Alexis.

"I'm Jeremiah Jackson," said Jeremiah Jackson, 'I picked up your vigilante, hitchhiking."

QUANTUM ROOTS II

"I think we have that much covered," said Alexis sipping ice water and popping a candy mint between her oval lips, "Let's move on to what happened, and let me remind everyone that what's said in this room, stays in this room."

"Yes ma'am," said Jackson.

"Of course," responded Jeremy.

Jeremiah Jackson was hauling computer hard--ware from Salem, New Hampshire to Bridgewater, New Jersey. Dinner time found the independent trucker two hours south of the Tappin Zee Bridge. Work traffic was heavy, truck stops scarce. Jackson eventually found an eatery with parking for a tractor trailer. Somehow, his routine dinner almost became his last supper.

"A waitress collaborated Jackson's story," said Alexis, "Two men followed Mr Jackson from the diner, into the parking lot. They were definitely desperado's of the third kind. Besides raid and rob, they were killers. We have an ID on the one who carried the weapon. He's wanted in three states for gunning down police officers. He would then use the press to highlight his distorted game of *cat and mouse*. He used the second man occasionally to fool federal agents who sought a lone assassin. In this case, robbery was the motive and our eye witness filled in the details."

KYLE   KEYES

The waitress had a window view of the whole incident while clearing off Jackson's counter dishes. The two men pulled Jackson from the cab before he could close the door. One man held a pistol to his head while the second man lifted his wallet. Then a man's shadow fell across the rumpled asphalt. It was the vigilante. The gunman swung his pistol toward the newcomer as two shots rang out. The first shot hit the gunman between the eyes. The second shot hit the second assailant in the left ear.

"I wonder why the vigilante always shoots people in the head,"   mused Jeremy Wade.

"Because he can,"   replied Alexis Grumman.

"Then what happened?"   asked Jeremy.

"Jeremiah peed his pants,"   said Alexis studying a facts sheet.

"I meant to go before I left the cafe"   explained the independent trucker speaking to Jeremy,   "Bladder isn't what it used to be, you know. Doctor says my prostate is choking off my urinal tract but those days are still ahead of you. And you won't be smiling when it numbs your sexual life."

"Something to look forward to,"   said Jeremy.

"The normal prostate is only walnut size,"   said Jeremiah Jackson,   "Mine is twice that large."

QUANTUM ROOTS II

"Interesting," said Jeremy.

"Can we get back to the vigilante," said Alexis.

"The guy in the black slicker?" asked Jackson.

"Yes, the guy in the black slicker."

"He changed to a guy in a brown slicker."

Alexis Grumman stared at Jeremiah Jackson who dropped another sugar cube into a complimentary cup of coffee. He added cream and stirred with a dirty forefinger. Asked Alexis, "You saw this change?"

"No ma'am," replied Jackson, "I squeezed to the back of my cab to change my shorts. Don't like to drive in wet jockeys."

"Of course," said an impatient Alexis, "And?"

"Anyway, when I got back up front," explained Jackson, "The guy standing outside my cab had on a brown coat. The hat and the gun belt were gone, and he was clutching a backpack."

"Same guy?" queried Alexis.

"Had to be," said Jackson, "We was the only folk people around."

"And he wanted a ride?" asked Alexis

"Had his thumb out," said Jackson, "I told him I was heading south. He said he was heading south. I said Bridgewater is my destination. He said that would work for him."

"You left the scene of a crime," said the DOA director.

"I wasn't gonna wait around any longer," said Jeremiah Jackson, "It's not my fault it takes so long for a cop to show up. Besides that, I wasn't the one doing the robbing, and I didn't shoot nobody."

"So what else did this hitchhiker say?" asked Alexis.

"Didn't talk much, but he was pretty sharp for a man who looked like he belonged on horseback."

"How's that ?"

"He told me I had a light out."

"So ?"

"He entered my truck on the passenger side," explained Jackson, "The blown bulb was the left tail light on my tractor. It's not obvious from the highway. Even the smokies miss it."

"So how did the vigilante know the bulb was out?" asked Alexis starting to show interest.

"He heard the left directional clicking faster than the right directional," replied Jackson, "That tells you there's a light out somewhere in the left side circuit. Frankly, your average hitchhiker isn't going to know this, unless he's a garage mechanic or some electronics nut."

"I see," said Alexis, "Did he say where he was headed?"

"South."

"We know that," curtly replied Alexis, "Where did you drop him off?"

"The intersection of 202 and 206," replied the big rig driver, "I said good luck and that quick he was gone. And just in time, too. The cops picked me up before I could head back uptown."

City police arrested Jeremiah in compliance with an all points bulletin, and then turned him over to a U.S. marshal who transported him to F.I.C. headquarters in Virginia. Jeremiah's cargo still set in the back end of his impounded, eighteen wheeler.

"I'm shit out of business if I can't get my truck back," said Jackson.

"You left a crime scene," repeated Alexis.

"We are talking about my livelihood," said the independent trucker.

"What are you chewing?" asked Alexis.

"Tobacco."

"You're chewing tobacco?"

"It's chewing tobacco," said Jeremiah Jackson, "Can't find it much in grocery stores, anymore. Have to find a tobacco shop. Wanna a wad?"

"No, I don't want a wad of chewing tobacco," snapped Alexis, "What I want is for you to stop spitting on the floor. Our janitor has enough to do cleaning up muddy footprints."

"Yes ma'am," said Jackson who paused to blow his nose into a giant handkerchief. He wadded up the polka dotted cloth, and stuffed the dirty linen into a trouser pocket before saying, "I didn't track that mud in here. See fer yourself. My boot bottoms shine like a baby's backside."

"I know that," said Alexis.

"You do?"

"Jeremy tracked the mud in," said Alexis.

"Oh," said Jackson, "What about my rig?"

"You left a crime scene," reminded Alexis for a third time, "You broke the law."

"But I am co operating," pointed out Jeremiah Jackson.

"I'll see what I can do," replied Alexis after a brief silence. Then, waving a pointer at the giant wall screen, she said, "Route 202 goes west, route 206 goes south."

"He went south," said Jackson, "He just ran through some evergreens and disappeared."

"What lies south?" asked Jeremy Wade.

QUANTUM ROOTS II

"South Jersey," said Alexis Grumman as Doug the invisible technician expanded monitor coordinates, "Shore points, the Pine Barrens and Hobbs Creek."

"Hobbs Creek !" cried Jeremy Wade, "Damn, Chapman's heading home."

"He's heading home," murmured Alexis.

"Do we bring in the locals?" asked Jeremy.

"Afraid so," conceded a frowning Alexis, "We are short handed right now, and I don't want you flying solo."

Chapter 13

Hobbs Creek, NJ

"Alvin, the newshounds are at the door," called in a female voice from the dispatch room, "I think they want a statement."

Hobbs Creek Police Chief, Alvin Phillips sat with a phone receiver in each ear. One handset was black, the other red. The black phone handled station business. The red phone took personal calls and any high level communication - real or imagined – that might come his way. Currently, a woman with Arabs in the attic was on the black phone, and Adam Quayle on the red line. Phillips bid *Arabs In The Attic* goodbye and put former police chief, Quayle on hold. Phillips then turned to face the open door to the adjoining room and cried, "Isabel, pretend not to notice the cameras, and keep your door locked."

"Alvin, how can I ignore a male tongue licking on the window glass."

"Isabel, I have no statement for the press at this time and you don't address me as Alvin," said Chief

Phillips, "My friends call me Phil and my employees address me as Chief Phillips."

"Alvin," replied township's first black dispatcher, "Your name is not Phil, your name is Alvin and if your name is Alvin then people should call you Alvin."

Chief Phillips groaned and spun in the squeaky swivel chair inherited from Benjamin Little, who inherited the seat from Adam Quayle, who inherited the territory from William Bo Brennan, who once out wrestled a grizzly bear – or so legend has it. The chair came to a stop facing the plate glass window that over-looked a parking lot of black and whites. Hobbs Creek has seen a fair amount of changes over the past half century. Police headquarters evolved from Bo Brennan's landmark farmhouse, to this steel and glass structure that now stands at the corner of Elm and Main. Millie's Meat Market gave way to a shopping mall just outside town limits. Otto's Farm And Garden bit the dust due to a highway by-pass that detoured prospective customers around the once popular fruit and vegetable mart.

Old Man Mayo's Esso is now an Exxon Mobil station with today's sticker shock prices that mark a sign of the times. And let us not forget Barney Kibble's taxi cab service that died when his mud caked, station wagon blew a rod in the mid-sixties. No one's sure what became of Barney – or his hearing aids – or the bumper sticker that read *I Like Ike*. Tri County Taxi replaced the one man operation with a slew of cabs that actually make an effort to stop for red lights.

Somethings never change.

Namely, little respect from a certain department *rank and file* member toward her Hobbs Creek, Police Chief – any police chief. Said Chief Phillips into the red phone, "And this Isabel Brown worked for you?"

"Jeeter Potts worked for me," replied ex Chief Adam Quayle, "We left together when town council adopted the Mandatory Retirement Act. After which, Chief Little took over. However, Isabel did train one year under Potts."

"Yes, I have a note on Jeeter Potts," said Chief Alvin Phillips, "How does a man remain a sergeant for fifty years?"

"Jeeter whittled away his career down at Fishers Pond," explained Adam Quayle, "He wanted to invent a car engine that would run on water, and Isabel's last name is Jackson, not Brown."

"It says Brown on her desk plaque."

Isabel Jackson was the former Isabel Brown who suffered a hearing loss while working for an upstate port authority. It was one of those *wrong place* at the *wrong time* things. As Isabel collected bridge fare, a wrinkled lady with a large bugle blew out her right ear drum. T'was the first of three mishaps to befall Isabel in a year's time. Her daughter got knocked up by a white boy, and her husband ran off with the boy's mother to audition for Dancing With The Stars.

Things brightened the following year. Isabel met Boa Beans Jackson who was a Lower Elk County lawyer. Beans wasn't much interested in chasing down the Mr. Brown, but his bespectacled eyes sparkled hearing the words, *port authority*. He married Isabel and kept her public name as Mrs Brown until after the pending trial. Thus far, the libel case had been delayed because port authority lawyers could not find a wrinkled lady with a large bugle.

Alvin Phillips gently set the phone receiver onto his desk pad. He stared at the mouthpiece. He ran thick fingers through his ruffled hair piece. He turned toward the plate glass window and watched a small dog cross Main Street, The dog stopped to pee on a fire house lamp post as Jeremy Wade entered the parking lot, below. Phillips quickly grabbed the still talking mouth-piece and barked, "The man you described just pulled in !"

"Good," said Adam Quayle.

KYLE KEYES

"And he knows the way to this resort ?" asked Phillips for verification.

"He's been there before," replied Quayle.

Police Chief Alvin Phillips strapped on a thirty eight and grabbed his trooper hat. He firmly believed that potential danger called for a stern image. He stuck his head through the dispatch door and said, "I'm on my way to Lake Powhatan."

"Ivy Chapman is in Cabin 18," said Isabel.

"I hope you were not eavesdropping," said the newly appointed police chief.

"Not me, suh."

"I'll take the back way out and don't let those reporters in."

"Yessuh and just for your information, Alvin," said Isabel Brown Jackson, "You have a streak of glue coming down your forehead."

*   *   *

"I'm Chief Phillips," said Alvin Phillips shaking hands with Jeremy Wade in the parking lot.

"I'm Jeremy Wade," said Jeremy Wade.

"I didn't know you federal agents traveled by motor scooter," said Phillips.

QUANTUM ROOTS II

The two men jumped aside as a school boy on a skate board careened off the special agent's mode of transportation. Phillips steadied his slippery hair piece, while Jeremy picked up the fallen two wheeler.

"This is not a motor scooter," said Jeremy.

"It looks like a scooter," said Alvin Phillips.

"This is a Super Bike," replied Jeremy, "Special Edition IV. This particular model is classified."

"It looks like a motor scooter," said Phillips.

"This baby will do zero to sixty in less than four seconds," said Jeremy, "Top speed is over 200mph. Has turbo boost, zero turn radius and blue tooth. You won't find many government agents flying around on one of these things."

"It flies?" asked Phillips.

"Sometimes," explained Jeremy Wade, "Other times I can't get the supersonic switch to work."

"Why does the license tag read *CALL 911 ?*" asked Alvin Phillips.

"Hop on," said Jeremy Wade, "I keep an extra helmet strapped to the luggage carrier."

"I spoke with a Lt General Grumman," said Alvin Phillips strapping on the head cover.

"My boss," confirmed Jeremy.

"Seems very stern."

"She spits on rattlesnakes," said Jeremy.

"Yes. .well. . This lady general wants this mission to go covert, from the way I get it," said Chief Phillips, "No backup, no air support, no news media."

"That's correct," said Jeremy, "Our job is to bring in Olan Chapman, dead or alive, regardless of public opinion or personal danger."

"I wish you wouldn't spin your service revolver like that ," said Alvin Phillips.

"We have to be ready," said Jeremy.

"I've never been on a covert mission before," said the police chief.

"This calls for a low profile," said Jeremy, "If we spook this guy, he'll disappear - or worse, revert to his alter ego."

"By that I take it you mean The Vigilante?"

"Yes, the vigilante," replied Jeremy.

"The gunman who aims for the head?"

"The same."

"There's a lot to be said for swat teams," said Alvin Phillips.

The road from Hobbs Creek to Lake Powhatan cuts across Route 91, runs another two miles north, and dead ends into the resort gates. The entire trek takes place within a twelve-square mile area charted off as

QUANTUM ROOTS II

Hobbs Creek Township.

"Agent Wade," suggested the chubby police chief in a loud voice to get over motor noise, "Would it help if I got off and walked."

"I have to throttle it down while transporting passengers," yelled back Jeremy, "Department policy to conform with insurance requirements."

"Of course," said Alvin Phillips, "I should have known that."

An earthy metamorphose takes place during the short journey to Lake Powhatan. Swamp cedars give way to oaks and scrub pines. Cattail sprouts change to thorny stalks. Mud to moss. Fishing takes a backseat to hunting, and a distant howl can often give a tender foot the jitters. Jeremy turned off the engine in order to hear the gate guard who was checking bumper stickers while on the phone.

"You must be the new police chief," said the guard looking at Alvin Phillips.

"And you must be Henry," said Phillips.

"You don't have a car?" asked the guard.

"I have a car," growled Alvin Phillips.

The entrance road to Lake Powhatan consisted of two lanes in, and one lane out. An overhang covered the inside lane to shelter the guard from sun and rain.

The low roof would accommodate passenger cars, but not high trucks. The guard checked out a large van in the outside lane, and then returned to say, "Not many scooters come through here."

"This is not a scooter," said Jeremy.

"Looks like a scooter," said the guard.

"We're here to see Ivy Chapman," broke in Alvin Phillips.

"You too ?" queried the guard.

You too ! Text ed in Alexis eavesdropping from FIC Headquarters, *Jeremy, who else is there !*

"The press came through here about an hour ago," said the guard answering Jeremy's relay of Alexis Grumman's question, "They wanted directions to Cabin Eighteen."

Damn, there must be a leak somewhere, Jeremy. Are they still in the park?"

"Are they still in the park?" relayed Jeremy

"Don't know," replied the gate guard, "I only check people in. They just drive out."

"They're not here," said Alvin Phillips.

"You're sure?" queried Jeremy.

"They're at police headquarters, downtown."

Jeremy ?

Listening.

QUANTUM ROOTS II

Seal off the entrance and enter with caution.

"We have a situation here," said Jeremy while flashing his ID at the guard, "Keep everybody out, but residents and those here on business."

"Yes Sir."

"Thank you," replied Jeremy, "And if anyone asks, this order comes from the United States Federal Investigation Center."

Better make that order a request, Jeremy. The northeast section of Lake Powhatan contains Indian burial plots that run into the Pinelands. We have limited authority there.

"Roger that," said Jeremy firing up the scooter, "Guard, change that order to a request."

"Are you sure you're a federal agent," said the gatekeeper watching the two men struggle to mount the scooter, "Can I see that badge again?"

*   *   *   *   *

Cabins surround Lake Powhatan like a wagon train. Most of these single story dwellings have a front porch, a tool shed outback and no garage. Some house year 'round residents. Others serve as a *get away* for those who would escape the monotony of daily work loads and pokey stop lights. Through July and August, this rustic retreat bustles with lazy fishermen and fast boats. Swimsuits hang from droopy clotheslines. Card players gather under the lakeside pavilion. And twice monthly, the VFW still drums up a square dance. Then by October, the happy waters return to dormancy as do the Island beaches a few miles to the southeast.

"I have my VFW card somewhere," said Alvin Phillips, "I'll have Ethel dig it out. Ethel loves to square dance."

Alexis, what is a square dance?

Google it, Jeremy.

Cabin Eighteen was put in backward so the living room would overlook the lake. Bedrooms faced the street. A stony driveway ran along a blind wall. The two lawmen left the scooter roadside and walked around to the rear.

"I never got past level two, myself," said Hobbs Creek's new police chief, "But Ethel danced all the way up to Level Four."

"Did you bring the warrant?" asked Jeremy.

"I thought you were taking care of that," said Alvin Phillips.

"We can't get a warrant without just cause," said Jeremy pulling on a cow bell, rope hung from the weathered front porch, "We're under the congressional gun now over phone privacy."

"I understand," said Alvin Phillips covering his ears while admiring the lakeside view. Most folks love the park grounds which are an oasis of nature. The fresh water lake sparkles like cut glass under bright skies. Oak trees flutter with robins come spring. Squirrels rob seed from handy bird feeders, while a bold mallard might peck at your screen door for stale bread crumbs. Asked Phillips, "So where are these rabbits coming from?"

"Chapman raises rabbits," explained Jeremy, "This bell is a dinner bell. They ring this bell and the rabbits come home to eat."

Soon, bunny rabbits covered the porch floor. Big rabbits. Little rabbits. Pink rabbits. White rabbits. Brown rabbits. Tri-colored rabbits.

"Maybe we should have rapped," suggested the police chief..

"I had to make sure any occupants hear us."

"I think they know we're here," said Phillips.

"I have a plan," said Jeremy.

"There's a rabbit nibbling on my sock," said Police Chief, Alvin Phillips.

"If Mrs Chapman answers," said Jeremy, "I will keep her occupied while you browse around. Don't let on you are searching. Pretend to get a drink of water or use the john."

"What if a man answers?" asked Phillips.

"Do not worry if the man is unarmed," replied Jeremy, "That man is Olan Chapman with a nature as mild as these rabbits."

"And if the man is armed," queried Phillips.

"Worry," said Jeremy. "That man will be Thee Vigilante."

"The vigilante who shoots people in the head," muttered Alvin Phillips.

"Yes," said Jeremy, "And he can shoot off your toupee before you see his hand move."

"How do you know I wear a piece?"

"Glue is running down your forehead," replied Jeremy.

Hobbs Creek Police Chief, Alvin Phillips pushed through the rabbit swarm and was about to bang on the solid wood door when Maryann Grundy rounded the corner – followed by fifty odd members who made up the neighborhood watch. One man carried a rather large bull horn. Blurted out Phillips, "Who the hell are you people ?"

Maryann Grundy lived next door to Ivy and Olan Chapman. They were not coffee clutch, but Maryann

QUANTUM ROOTS II

was block captain and head of the Citizens For Action group. She was appointed to that position by peers who go north following Labor Day and return after Memorial Day. Maryann stayed put year around and thus made a good lookout. Also, Maryann had roots here. She was daughter to Tom and Angel Grundy who owned Cabin 20 back in the Fifties. Upon her parents death, Maryann inherited the lakeside property when her twin sister moved to San Diego.

Often, the eager Maryann would jump the gun in her zest to be a good block captain. Earlier on this day, Maryann spotted the final reporter snooping around.. She mistook the newshound for a prowler. After calling state police, she notified her first lieutenant who made the first of two pyramid calls. Each of those recipients then called two more people who called two more people, etc, etc. Now a small army stood behind Cabin Eighteen.

"STAND DOWN," blared the bull horn, "THE AUTHORITIES ARE ON THEIR WAY!"

"I am the authorities," said Alvin Phillips.

"We know Chief Benjamin Little," countered Maryann Grundy, "And you are not him."

Alexis, get us out of this, text ed Jeremy. *Contact somebody, contact everybody !*

KYLE KEYES

"THIS IS A CITIZEN'S ARREST," blared the bull horn, "YOU ARE BEING CHARGED WITH BURGLARY, IMPERSONATING A POLICE OFFICER AND CARRYING A FIREARM."

"Burglary !" screamed Alvin Phillips, "We are not stealing anything !"

"YOU ARE STEALING RABBITS !"

"What!"

"WE HAVE WITNESSES !"

Alexis, get us out of this !! re-texted Jeremy.

Damn, I think the computers just went down, text ed back a smiling General Alexis Grumman.

_____

Chapter 14

Ivy Chapman peeked through parted curtains, as Maryann Grundy and the CFA, herded Jeremy Wade and Alvin Phillips off the cabin porch. Once the two lawmen disappeared from sight, Ivy breathed a sigh of relief and eased back to her video phone. A loose rabbit appeared from nowhere and nearly tripped the stocky woman as she grabbed the *smart* phone from the sink counter.

"What's going on?" said the phone.

"Olan," whispered Ivy, "Where are you?"

"Nearby."

"Well, you get your ass home here."

"Ivy, I can't," said the whiskered face on the cell phone screen, "Feds are everywhere and stop kicking the rabbit."

"Can I meet you somewhere?" asked Ivy.

"No."

The Chapmans first met at an Orange County bar in Kissimmee, Florida. They were in the Orlando area to visit Walt Disney's Animal Kingdom. The year was 2004.

Six named hurricanes blew through the Sunshine State in less than three months. Floridians were frightened. You could see the apprehension in taunt faces at food markets, gas stations, supply centers where home owners flocked to buy bottled water and plywood. News media suggested that the Sunshine State be renamed the hurricane state. One isolated email wanted to move Florida north to Alaska.

Hurricane Charlie was the second blow of that busy season. Charlie came ashore at Punta Gorda, raged through Zolfo Springs and stormed into Orange County before moving north. Winds clocked between 110 and 150 mph. State damages reached 13 billion, plus. Charlie also spawned sudden tornadoes, closed down Disney's Animal Kingdom, and landed Olan Chapman on a bar stool next to Ivy Ann Goya.

"I should have listened to mama," lamented Ivy, "She told me to stay out of bars."

They married in a fever hotter than a jalapeno pepper. They designated Hurricane Charley as their best man, and set up housekeeping in a Buffalo City condo near where Olan worked. Two pay raises later, they bought a split level in Hyde Park, not far from Niagara Falls. Then the job market crashed and the slender computer wizard moved his wife and two pet rabbits to this rustic cabin in Lower Elk County, New Jersey. Now, several years later, the Chapmans were mortgage heavy, money light and still childless. Only the rabbits were flourishing.

"Olan, your freaking rabbits are everywhere," cried Ivy Chapman in a voice growing louder, "And what's this shit about you being a vigilante. You never fired a gun in your life."

"I fired a potato gun, once."

"Olan, you couldn't hit a bull in the ass with a ping pong paddle," said Ivy, "Do these government agents know you are suicidal?"

"I'm not suicidal."

"Olan, you have been over the Falls twice."

"They were not suicide attempts," said Olan Chapman, "I was crusading for a worthwhile cause."

"Olan, nobody goes over Horseshoe Falls to raise public awareness of male dysfunctional disorder."

"Ivy, I have a problem."

"Olan, don't tempt me."

"I keep turning into someone else."

"What !" cried Ivy

"It almost like a metamorphose," explained Chapman, "I become another person. And I get head aches."

"Olan, you're drinking again."

"Ivy, I'm not drinking."

"Are these phones tapped," asked Ivy.

"No," replied the slender computer wizard, "I mailed you a new phone with a fresh identity."

"In that case," barked Ivy Chapman, "You get your bony ass back home here."

"Ivy, the guy on the scooter was a fed."

"You don't know that, Olan."

"I watched him leave police headquarters."

"Olan."

"Yes?"

"Jeeter calls almost daily to see how you are."

"Potts?"

"Jeeter Potts is your best friend," whimpered Ivy, suddenly going from bitter to sweet, "He misses you, I miss you, the rabbits miss you."

*   *   *   *   *

America's most wanted man powered off his cell phone. He sat by Fishers Pond in nearby Hobbs Creek. He muttered something inaudible to a nosy mallard, and skipped pebbles across the shiny blue water. He couldn't help but recall happier days, when he and partner Jeeter Potts, would dominate pinocle action every Tuesday night. Games were held at the Hobbs Creek Firehouse. Chapman and Potts were masters at running down two suits. They knew the bids, held the Hobbs Creek record for slam hands, and won the Firehouse Tourney, three times running.

They were the glory days for Olan - those five minutes in the sun that we all seek. He became the talk of the town and proudly wore a red and white button that read, Card Player Of The Year.

Then came the car accident, the head concussion followed by the metamorphose, which led to gun play and multiple slayings. After which, the geeky computer wizard rocketed back into the limelight, but for all the wrong reasons. Consequently, he could not go home again.

He frowned at the whiskered face in Fishers Pond that frowned back. He was tired and hungry. He needed a bath. His wavy locks were black and brown from a self performed dye job. He tested the pond water before washing, not being one to jump in.

Olan Chapman's former years read like a Charlie Brown cartoon – mild mannered, passive, timid. Now, faced with danger, Olan could feel the change occur. His blue eyes would turn black, watery legs stabilize, voice deepen. The metamorphose was unnerving for sure, but even more scary, Olan was beginning to like this new person more than he liked himself. And that was frightening.

He reached for his cell phone to recall wife Ivy, changed his mind and skipped a pebble across Fishers Pond. He reached for the phone again, changed his mind and bounced another stone off the still waters. An hour later, he grabbed his backpack and caught a ride out of town.

Chapter 15

Everyone loves a parade - for sure. New Orleans can attest to that. Two million fun lovers visit Louisiana each year to taste the flavor of Mardi Gras, also known as Fat Tuesday. The celebration holds religious vibes for many. Others are curiosity seekers. Jeremy Wade was here to follow up on a vigilante sighting.

What do we have? texted Alexis.

So far, nothing, texted back Jeremy as a float of purple dragons rolled by.

Jeremy, did that girl flash you.

What girl ?

You are supposed to be working the Uptown section, Jeremy. I think you are prowling around on Bourbon Street.

I'll bring you a string of beads.

Jeremy, I can get beads at the dollar store.

Alexis, these are glass beads. .from the 1950's .made in Czechoslovakia.

Historians believe the first Louisiana, Mardi Gras took place in March, 1699, when french explorers set up camp just south of what is now, New Orleans. That precise day was being celebrated back in Paris as Fat Tuesday. Thus, these explorers threw a small gala and dubbed the spot as Point Du Mardi Gras. Over the years, those humble roots have grown into masquerade balls, king cake parties, organized parades and throws, which are mostly beads, small toys and doubloons. Today there is a growing fad for young women to expose their breasts as a lure to catch the more pricy throws.

I'll be checking for topless girls, Jeremy.
I think I spotted our mark, Alexis.
I'll be checking for topless girls, Jeremy.
This is for real, Alexis.

Jeremy was halfway uptown when he spotted a man dressed as yesteryear's federal, marshal service. The man wore a badge shaped as a five-pointed star. The outer ring read, United States Marshal.

Is he wearing black? texted Alexis.
From his boots to his flat brim stetson.
Jeremy, try not to embarrass the agency.

Special Agent, Jeremy Wade caught up with his target just as Pete Fountain's Half Fast Walking Club passed by at a half fast pace. Said Jeremy, "They're on their way to the French Quarter."

"I know that," replied the suspect, "I come here every year."

"I like your costume, Olan," said Jeremy.

"My wife sews," said the suspect, "And how do you know my name is Olan?"

"I'm a federal agent," said Jeremy flashing his ID card, "You have the right to remain silent."

"You are kidding," said the suspect, "I'm afraid I'm not who you think I am."

"We have met before," said Jeremy.

"I don't think so," said the suspect, "And I wish you wouldn't spin a gun like that, it could go off."

"You need to know I've been long hours on the practice range since our last showdown," said Jeremy.

"What showdown?"

"Pistols in the Pinelands."

"Wasn't that a movie?" smiled the suspect.

"You shot the snaps off my snow suit."

"And your pants fell down?"

"They did," replied Jeremy.

"You have the wrong man," said the suspect.

"You have the right to an attorney," said Jeremy slapping on the handcuffs.

'This is just a costume," said the suspect "I'm only pretending to be the vigilante."

"I don't think so," said Jeremy, "I picked up on that small hitch in your walk. I have a keen eye for small details like that."

"I don't walk with a hitch," said the suspect.

"If you can't afford a lawyer," said Jeremy, "The court will appoint one for you."

"Jeremy, we need some further ID," said Alexis breaking in over the two way, "Put his thumb print against the screen face on your communicator."

Sometime later, forensics reported that the print belonged to one Olin Clapman, a city councilman from Lower Elk County, N.J.

"Sorry," said Jeremy removing cuffs, "I'll buy you a snow cone."

"I can use this incident as a story for my grand children," said Clapman sitting curbside and licking purple ice, "Otherwise, you would be close to a lawsuit and I think your phone is calling."

"Yes," said Jeremy, "I'm afraid it is."

Jeremy, you are neither fish nor foul. Your job is to merely find Chapman. After which, you call me and I send the proper authorities.

Yes Ma'am.

And, you don't confide to Stanley the doorman that I wear pink panties !"

QUANTUM ROOTS II

You heard about that ?

The whole building heard about that !

Are we in trouble?

General Taylor wants to see the two of us when you get back.

Chapter 16

Olan Chapman just barely caught the last west-bound freight out of Barstow, which is located midway between Los Angeles and Las Vegas. Barstow is to the Inland Empire, what early Rome was to Italy. This busy transportation center consists of four major highways and a giant rail yard owned by Burlington Northern Santa Fe. Chapman's last car ride brought him here from Flagstaff. He was thumb weary, leg tired and ready for a nap. He ran up the embankment from Agate Rd to the tracks overhead, and tossed his pack back through an open boxcar door.

Then, he stumbled reaching for the rusty handle bar that served as a mounting grip.

The train was over a hundred cars long, with four diesels up front and two in the rear. As the lead diesel rounded Community Curve, the engineer blew the horn and the train picked up speed.

Chapman jumped up and scampered over loose bedrock and protruding railroad ties. Cursing, he caught up with the open door and swung aboard to find a hobo digging into the runaway backpack.

QUANTUM ROOTS II

"That's my bag ! " cried Chapman.

"Don't mean no harm," said the stubble faced drifter, "Just browsing."

"Well, this is not a sales outlet," snapped Olan snatching his cell phone from the drifter, "Has this thing been vibrating long?"

"Vibrating ?"

"Shaking."

"I didn't do nuttin to it, mister. . .honest."

Olan Chapman flipped open the phone and said, "Are you on the new phone?"

"Olan, where are you?" cried Ivy Chapman.

"Are you on the new phone !"

"I'm on the new phone," confirmed Ivy, "Now where the hell are you ?"

"I can't talk now," said Olan.

"We are on our way to Bakersfield," replied the drifter, eavesdropping.

"Who was that?" asked Ivy.

Chapman stared at his newly acquired traveling partner and frowned. The drifter wore a dirty tuxedo, a soiled white shirt and a bright red bow tie. His emerald eyes looked water logged. He rigidly clung to a fresh wine bottle wrapped in a paper bag with a twisted top. Said Olan to Ivy, "Some hobo down on his luck."

"I'm not a hobo," said the drifter, "I am Sir Edward O'Toole the magician. I do magic tricks. Maybe you caught my last act. I just finished a gig at Caesars."

"I came west via Route 40," said Olan by way of explanation. Then, Olan said to Ivy, "I told you not to call me unless it's an emergency. We can't afford to keep buying burners."

"This is an emergency," cried Ivy, "Your rabbits have moved out onto the highway. State police are threatening to call in the national guard. You need to get your bony ass home."

"Rabbits?" chipped in the drifter, "I could use a rabbit in my next act. I have a gig coming up out on the coast."

"I can't come home," said Chapman talking to his wife, "Not yet anyway."

"I'll swap you some wine for a rabbit," said the hobo.

"I owe you," said Olan taking the bottle from the drifter.

"Olan, you're not supposed to be drinking," said Ivy, "You know you get suicidal when you drink."

"I'm not suicidal," whispered Chapman into the phone, "I'm a fugitive. Our house is under watch. Our relatives are under watch. Our friends are under watch."

"Then wear a disguise," said Ivy Chapman.

"I have a disguise."

"Olan, your Wyatt Earp garb is not a disguise."

"Just remember to feed the rabbits."

"Screw the rabbits," replied Ivy Chapman in a resigned voice.

"Really," said the hobo.

The Tehachapi Loop loomed into view when real trouble boarded the mile long freight. As the train slowed to maneuver a sharp curve, two jail birds from Tijuana came through the open, boxcar door. Cried one escapee as he spotted the brown paper bag, "I think we just found ourselves a drink, Hobie."

"We don't want any trouble," said Edward O Toole, now holding the wine bottle.

"They don't want no trouble, Butch," mocked the escapee named Hobie.

"But we need a drink," sneered the one named Butch, "And we can use that outfit he's wearing when we get to the tables."

"Leave him alone," said Olan.

"You stay out of this!" barked the larger man.

The two convicts were Robert Butch Cleaver, and Herbert Hobie Howel. They were serving life sentences for smuggling cocaine into Mexico. They escaped from a Tijuana road gang and re entered the states by hijacking a cab. Howell stole the drivers cap and ID, while Cleaver kept the driver muzzled in the trunk. Authorities have yet to find the cab or the driver.

"You're headed the wrong way," said Chapman "Las Vegas is northeast of here."

"Dammit Butch," cried Hobie, "I told you we hopped the wrong train!"

"Shut up, Hobie!" growled the larger convict, who then cursed out Olan Chapman and began to attack Sir Edward O'Toole. Soon, Butch Cleaver and Herbert Howel discovered that determination can come in small packages. O'Toole refused to give up the wine. The ex-circus performer curled into a fetal position and clutched the oval bottle to his bosom like a halfback running off tackle. Cleaver stepped back and ran hairy fingers over his bald head. A faded tattoo that read LOVE covered his right forearm. Teeth flashed silver as he sneered, "I think this piss-ant needs a dose of the same medicine we gave that cab driver."

"I like it," said Hobie, who had calmly munched on a hamburger while Cleaver stomped their puny cab driver to death, just south of San Diego City. The two fugitives then dumped the body into a waste container along US Route 5. The cab driver was reported missing in Tijuana, but not in the States. Chuckled Hobie as Cleaver raised a menacing boot over O'Toole, "This is what we call getting the boot."

"You took Route 5 out of San Diego?" cut in Olan Chapman peeking at his hidden cell phone, "Who made that bonehead decision?"

All activity stopped.

"How does he know we took Route 5 out of San Diego," said the smaller convict.

"I told you to shut the fuck up," barked Cleaver at Chapman.

"If you would have taken Route 15," continued Chapman, "You two assholes would be in Vegas right now."

Butch Cleaver flushed angry red. He turned away from O'Toole and spit at Olan Chapman. Cried Cleaver, "Who the hell are you calling an asshole !"

"I'm looking at you, dumb ass," said Chapman, as the wine took effect, "Drug runners don't smuggle cocaine into Mexico. The stuff goes north, not south."

And just like that, Robert Butch Cleaver lost it. He collared Chapman and tossed the computer geek off the train, bag and baggage. Then, Cleaver threw the magician out the boxcar door, with his attire still on, but without the wine bottle. The two men rolled down the tree studded embankment, where Olan collided with a stubborn evergreen trunk, and O'Toole bumped heads with a rather large boulder.

"You okay?" asked Olan looking around as he checked his own body for cuts and injuries.

Edward O'Toole lay motionless.

Olan cursed and began crawling toward O'Toole when the metamorphose started. Panic gave way to an eerie calm. His shaky legs steadied. His nervous blue eyes turned to a hollow black stare.

Overhead, the monstrous freight train rumbled across the top rails of Tunnel Nine. Soon, it would pass beneath itself.

Olan Chapman reached for his backpack.

Chapter 17

The Tehachapi Loop is an engineering feat of a time gone by. A time when railroads were boss, and any one who was anyone, either worked for the railroad, or knew someone who worked for the railroad-unless they were a politician or a movie star.

Southern Pacific Railroad built the Loop in 1876 to help longer freight trains over the Tehachapi Pass. Loop elevation rises a steady 2% grade and gains a whopping 77 ft in elevation from entrance to exit. Trains over 4000 feet long, actually pass over themselves while going around the loop.

Robert Butch Cleaver and Herbert Howel now sat in the door opening of the boxcar. Their feet dangled downward, their mood ticked upward as they passed the wine bottle back and forth. They could see the freight cars rumble overhead as their boxcar entered the east side of Tunnel Nine.

"You wanna hear sumptin funny?" said Cleaver as all went black.

"Lay it on me," replied Hobie Howel.

"The railroad owes us."

"How's that, Butch?"

"We threw two hobos off their train."

"I like it," chuckled Hobie, "I like it."

Laughter ceased as the boxcar pulled out in the daylight.

"Who the hell's that," said Hobie Howel.

"I don't know," replied Butch Cleaver, "Looks like Wyatt Earp."

"Maybe it's Bat Masterson," said Howel.

The vigilante stood just shy of the bend in the tracks. Feet spread. Flat brim hat tilted. His right hand hung loose just below the holster.

"I don't like this, Butch," muttered Hobie.

A windy howl blew fumes back into the tunnel. Clacking wheels continued to pass overhead. Skies turned dark. Up front, a horn blew as the boxcar with the open door rumbled toward the figure in black.

"Hey you," cried Robert Cleaver slowly rising upward with a forced chuckle, "I know you. You're Doc Holiday, right?"

No reply came.

Cleaver began to laugh.

Howel dropped the empty wine jug.

The vigilante waited for the occupied box car to draw closer.

QUANTUM ROOTS II

Both fugitives were now on their feet, framed in the doorway. Robert Cleaver nudged Hobie Howel who began to laugh. Both men were belly laughing when the bullet hit Cleacer between the eyes. The second shot entered Howel's right ear, and took off his left ear coming out.

Both men fell backward as the westbound freight passed the vigilante and rumbled toward Bakersfield.

Blood gradually soaked the boxcar floor.

Chapter 18

F.I.C. Headquarters:

Alexis Grumman paused for an ice water drink. She popped a fresh mint between her oval lips. She had Doug bring up another view of Tehachapi Loop on the big screen, then resumed questioning Edward O'Toole.

"Ma'am, with all respect to your uniform," said the magician, "It's Sir Edward, not Edward."

"Of course," replied Alexis, "We need to know whether the vigilante went east or west. . .Sir Edward."

"I already told you," said O'Toole, "The man I saw went east."

"He boarded the next freight going around the Loop and headed east?" asked Alexis for verification.

"That's what I saw, ma'am."

Alexis walked to room center and extended an adjustable pointer. She tapped earth imagery projected on the giant screen, saying, "This is the ground area on the west side of Tunnel Nine. We found you lying against this boulder. You were conscious, but in need of some minor first aid."

QUANTUM ROOTS II

"That's where I landed when the hobos threw me off the train," said O'Toole.

"Hobos, meaning the fugitives?"

"Yes ma'am, the convicts."

The dead bodies of Robert Cleaver and Herbert Howel were discovered when the freight train reached Bakersfield. The engineer remembered seeing a black garbed figure standing track side, back at the Tehachapi Loop. Local police contacted Federal authorities.

Asked Alexis, "Why were you still sitting there when Agent Wade showed up ?"

"I was waiting for a train," replied O'Toole.

"Yes . .well . .amusing."

"I bet you've never hopped a train."

"No, Sir Edward, I've never hopped a train."

"Well, the Loop isn't New York City, ma'am," explained O'Toole, "I had to wait for a freight going west. Then, I had to wait for an open boxcar door. I'm getting a bit old to be riding rooftop."

"Yes," said Alexis. Then moving on, "I can't find data on a Sir Edward O'Toole working a magic act in Las Vegas. Exactly, where did you perform?"

"Mostly on the strip," replied O'Toole.

" I assume you mean Las Vegas Boulevard," said Alexis, "Could you be more specific. Did you perform at Caesars, Cosmopolitan, Encore ?"

"Mostly, I worked Castaways and Frontier."

Alexis Grumman stared long and hard at Edward O'Toole. She nodded her head *no* as she scrolled down a hand-held device, "I'm afraid you're not a very good liar, Sir Edward."

"Ma'am ?"

"Castaways was demolished in January 2006, and the New Frontier came down the following year, on November 13, 2007 , which is roughly a decade ago," said Alexis tapping the small screen, "I have the data right here. . .so . . .maybe you would like to rethink your story."

Edward O'Toole sat at a small coffee table used for breaks in the screening room. His eyes dropped to study a bran muffin as he asked, "Could I have another one of these?"

"Of course," said Alexis lifting a glass cover.

"These are good," said O'Toole.

"Yes they are," replied Alexis.

"They keep me regular."

"They keep us all regular," replied Alexis.

"I'm not really a magician," admitted Edward O'Toole, "I just wear this outfit so people won't think I'm a hobo."

QUANTUM ROOTS II

"Well, you had me fooled," said Jeremy coming back from the kitchen with fresh coffee.

"It fools most people," said O'Toole, "And it cuts down on vagrancy arrests."

Alexis returned to room center and said, "Let's recap. You said that you awoke and saw a figure in black, board an eastbound train."

"That's what I said."

"It was a man?"

"It was a man."

"Doug, keep the topography and bring up the two ID photos on the split screen," said Alexis.

Inset pictures of Olan Chapman and the vigilante flashed on screen corners. Alexis tapped the photo of the vigilante and asked for verification.

"That's the man that boarded the eastbound," confirmed O'Toole, and then quickly added, "But I've never seen the other man."

"That's strange," said Alexis.

"Ma'am?"

"We found Olan Chapman's fingerprints on the boarding handle," said Alexis, "So we know he was inside that boxcar with you, and we have to believe the fugitives threw you both off the train."

"Am I under arrest?" asked Edward O'Toole.

"Not yet, but you might want to rethink your story a second time," said Alexis tapping the map area where O'Toole lost consciousness, "From this view point, you could have witnessed the whole shooting."

"Ma'am, Olan Chapman saved my life."

"Mr O'Toole, Chapman is wanted for murder on multiple counts."

"They were going to kill me."

"Edward, this is not a vagrancy charge," said Alexis in a somewhat softer tone, "We're talking aiding and abetting someone wanted for murder. We're talking a prison term."

Silence.

"I called dispatch for Kern County," said Alexis running the pointer over the large screen to show how double tracks in Keene, reduce to a single track to pass through Tunnel Nine, "There was no eastbound train waiting for track clearance. There was a freight on the Walong siding, but this train was going west. I think you can see the problem."

More silence.

"You are in over your head," warned the female general which prompted the real story to come out. Bit by bit. between coffee sips, and huge bites into bran muffins, O'Toole told of the boxcar confrontation that led to his getting tossed from the train, and losing consciousness. However, he did wake in time to witness Olan Chapman experiencing metamorphose. The eye color changed. Olan's demeanor became aggressive. His walk picked up a swagger. Asked Alexis, "Where did the gun come from?"

"Out of the backpack."

"And the hat?"

"Backpack."

"Doug, bring up all the shots we have of Olan Chapman and the vigilante," called out Alexis.

"You want the Jesse Joe Jacks pictures?" asked the invisible projectionist, "Or just the current film of Chapman and Leroy McCoy?"

"Everything," said Alexis, "Past and present."

Soon, a hundred pictures filled the big screen. Some fuzzy and some clear. Some depicted Chapman as Jesse Joe Jacks, a county game warden, and Korean War vet. The newer ones showed Chapman as Samuel Leroy McCoy, a deputy marshal from 1876 Dodge City, Kansas.

"What strikes you about these pictures," asked Alexis of Edward O'Toole.

"Ma'am?"

"What stands out about these photographs?"

KYLE KEYES

Sir Edward O'Toole polished off the last muffin and looked back to the big screen. He wiped up some spilled coffee with his shirt sleeve, apologized, thanked Alexis for the snack and said, "I'm not very good at puzzles, ma'am."

"Well, the first vigilante shot left handed and the current vigilante shoots right handed," said Jeremy Wade trying to be helpful."

"Yes, that is a bit inconsistent," admitted Alexis, "But let's look at something that's very consistent. The vigilante always dresses in black, but Olan Chapman wears nothing but brown. How does he do that?"

Edward O'Toole began to chuckle.

"This is funny ?" asked Alexis.

"I was there to see the metamorphose."

"And ?"

"He simply turned his clothes inside out."

"Damn !" cried Alexis smacking forehead with an open palm, "Reversible s! He's wearing reversible s! We never thought of reversible s."

"Am I free to go, now?" asked O'Toole.

"Reversible s," murmured the female general in trance like tones

"Yes ma'am, I watched him turn that riding coat inside out."

"One last item," said Alexis, "Which way did Chapman go, east or west ?"

"Neither," replied O'Toole, "He headed north toward Route 58."

"Thank you for being helpful," said Alexis.

"And while I'm bean spilling," said Sir Edward O'Toole, "There is one more thing."

"I'm listening."

"On the trip here, Agent Wade ran into a drone over the interstate. Packages flew every where."

"You need to forget that, Sir Edward."

"I almost fell off the back end of his scooter."

"Agent Wade's scooter is classified."

"I didn't know motor scooters could fly."

"You are dismissed, Sir Edward."

"Yes, Ma'am."

Chapter 19

Later at DPA Headquarters:

"Ma'am, it's time to turn out the lights," called out the projectionist, "We are in danger of becoming pumpkins."

"Doug, what does Chapman's reversible clothes tell you?" asked Alexis.

"Boss, you have been staring at that screen all night," replied the weary projectionist, "Chapman's garb tells us he's wearing clothes under that slicker. So, we know he's not a flasher. Also, too much luminous light can give you *surfer's eye.*"

"I just got off the phone with Dr Dearwood," said Alexis, "These reversible s are significant. They tell us that Olan Chapman knows who he is, and what he's doing. Dearwood has never believed that Olan was truly suicidal. If he were, quote unquote, he'd be dead by now. More likely, Dearwood claims that Chapman needs to prove that he's not afraid to die. But to do that, he has to live."

QUANTUM ROOTS II

"A strange paradox," agreed the projectionist, "Prove it to who?"

"Prove it to the world," said Alexis, "Prove it to himself. Dearwood traces this obsession back to childhood days when Olan ran and hid in the face of danger."

"So who are we after," asked the projectionist switching off the lights, "Chapman, Jacks or McCoy?"

"We're chasing a man on a mission," replied Alexis, "Also, a man who's a loose cannon. Dearwood predicts that whenever trouble arises, Olan Chapman will jump right in the middle."

"With his reversible garb?"

"Yes, with his reversible garb," said a thoughtful Alexis, "So, maybe we need to rethink these reversible s. Maybe dressing like someone he once was, adds fuel to this metamorphose. They say clothes make the man. This could be such the case."

"Goodnight, Boss."

"Goodnight Doug. . .and Doug?"

"Yes ma'am?"

"I don't surf," smiled Alexis, "Army brats don't grow up with surf boards."

"I was referring to web surfing," explained the invisible projectionist.

"Of course," said the lady general as the screen went blank, "And you're right, Doug. I am tired. Jim had me on the carpet most of the night."

"Jim?"

"General Taylor."

"I'm surprised Taylor hasn't transferred Agent Wade to another agency by now," said the invisible technician, "Everybody in the building knows that you and Jeremy sleep together. . . if you will pardon me for saying so .. . anyway, from I hear, the general takes a dim view on inner department affairs."

"We reached a compromise," sighed Alexis.

"Who reached a compromise?"

"The general and myself."

"Really."

"Sometimes, we have to give up something to get something, Doug."

"You didn't."

"I did," admitted Alexis.

"You mean Old Ironhorse finally got to see the pink panties?"

"Yes, and now I know how he got the nickname, Ironhorse."

"Damn," whistled the invisible technician, "So when you said the general had you on the carpet, you mean he had you on the carpet?"

"I mean he had me on the carpet."

"Does Jeremy know?"

"No."

Chapter 20

Post Easter brought multiple vigilante sightings to Carlton City, California. U.S. Marshal, Leroy McCoy appeared everywhere. Or so it seemed. As though some one hung a sign out that read: *Vigilante Stop Here.* Soon, back alleys became safer to walk. Robberies and rapes fell a whopping 85 per cent. Many, even left their doors unlocked after dark.

News media enjoyed a field fire.

Social media kept the fire burning.

Clothesline talk sizzled.

Consequently, more change followed. As Leroy McCoy's fan club grew, Olan Chapman joined the ranks of *most wanted* for murder on multiple counts. Thus, Alexis Grumman persuaded General James Taylor to transfer the case from DPA to IC (Intelligence Central.) Grumman stated her case on two facts: IC had more manpower for the job; and the vigilante sightings were no longer a paranormal event.

The DPA exclusion would be short lived. Alexis was one toe into a hot bath when a late phone call summoned her back to F.I.C. Headquarters.

QUANTUM ROOTS II

"Olan Chapman took a bullet to the chest at point blank range," boomed James Taylor from behind a desk bigger than a bread truck, "And . .we . have. . no . . body."

"No body?"

"No body," repeated the five star general, "All we have is a film clip that came from a patron's camera phone. Details are still coming in, but we know there was no body when the locals arrived at the scene."

"I see," said Alexis studying a fast film clip playing out on Taylor's media screen. Olan Chapman could be seen taking a chest bullet that sent the slender computer wizard reeling backward through a California nightclub door. The shooter was not shown. Witnesses said that local authorities searched the building and surrounding premises for the victim, but came up empty.

"So when did all this happen, Jim?"

"Earlier this afternoon," replied Taylor, "After which, another vigilante sighting occurred just outside of Fresno. Consequently, the news media is now talking wormholes again. Someone even posted the clip on social media."

"We have already ruled out wormholes," said Alexis.

"So how do we explain the vigilante sighting that followed the shooting?"

"No doubt a copycat," replied Alexis.

"But that is Olan Chapman in this news clip?" asked James Taylor mostly for verification.

"That's our boy," replied Alexis.

"So where's the body?" mused Taylor.

"What about blood?" asked Alexis, "There had to be some blood."

"No blood," replied Taylor.

"Damn this case," muttered Alexis staring out a top level window. She left an empty water bottle on the giant size desk, and returned to the window to say, "I never realized you could see interstate headlights from this office, until recently."

"We never had a nightcap until recently," said Taylor, "I was hoping for more nightcaps like that."

Alexis Grumman turned from the window to face the five star general, and as his eyes said *yes*, her eyes said *no*. She read the disappointment in his face. Her voice softened to say, "Jim, I am sorry."

"I don't want sorry, Alexis."

"I know what you want, Jim. . .but. . .I do have a gentleman friend. . and what happened the other night, should not have."

"By gentleman friend, you mean Agent Jeremy Wade," boomed Taylor.

"Yes sir."

"The Jeremy Wade who drove a car over a cliff into a gravel pit?"

"He was in a bad snow storm, Sir."

"The Agent Wade who blew up an army jeep?"

"His aim was a bit off in the grenade toss," said Alexis, "I have to admit that."

James Taylor gave Alexis Grumman a long stare, before asking, "Is it my after shave lotion ?"

"Jim, you know I'm a cougar," said Alexis.

"Yes, I know that," replied a resigned James Taylor, "Just my luck."

"It could be worse," said Alexis.

"How's that?" queried Taylor.

"You could be an officer and a gentleman."

The two generals shared a common laugh. Alexis buzzed for coffee delivery while the top general took a classified late night call. Getting no response on the coffee, Alexis strode to the kitchen, and returned with two black coffee's and a stirring spoon. Said Alexis, "Still keep that bottle in your desk drawer?"

"Does Tarzan chase Jane," smiled General James Ironhorse Taylor, pouring a shot of whiskey into each cup, "I talked to every IC department head, Alexis. You will get full cooperation as field commander for this operation. You can figure on thirty agents."

"That's triple the manpower I had for Operation *Quick Draw*," whistled Alexis Grumman referring to the East Coast dragnet which netted nothing, "We must be getting serious about Olan Chapman."

"National headlines demand it," explained the top brass man, "And this time we stay with our agenda. Nobody drifts back to their home unit until we nab our target."

"Even if he disappears?" queried Alexis.

"Especially if he disappears," said James Taylor, "That's why we have a Department for Paranormal Activities."

The two generals tapped coffee cups in a toast to the *old guard*. Alexis then said, "Don't blame your aftershave lotion, Jim. Blame it on the Bossa Nova."

"I won't stop trying, Alexis."

"I'd be disappointed if you did," replied Alexis.

Chapter 21

Olan Chapman sat on a saggy cot and took a swig of rum from an open bottle - still wrapped in a shopping bag. He peeled off boots and socks. He took two more swigs. His chest hurt from a gunman's point blank firepower. His feet ached from the long trek from Carlton City, to this dingy motel just outside of Fresno.

He started to call wife Ivy, changed his mind and took another mouthful of rum. He knew the feds would eventually track down her new phone number. He finished the rum, muttered *hell with the feds*, and reached for the phone.

"Ivy, you should have been there."

"Olan, where are you !"

"I told that bastard what he could do with his freaking gun."

"Olan, are you drinking?"

"He was terrorizing the patrons, Ivy," burped the slender computer wizard, "Well, that all stopped when I walked in. . I wanna tell you . ."

"Olan, you are drinking again !"

KYLE KEYES

"He pointed that gun right in my face . . and. .I pointed my chin right in his face. . ."

"Olan, you promised to stop drinking !"

"You had to be there, Ivy . . .you had to see the look on that bastard's face when I told him to shove his gun up his ass."

The confrontation took place at a gentleman's club just north of Carlton, Ca. Two male patrons began a verbal battle over a young female stripper. As the club bouncer stepped in, a fourth man pulled a revolver and all fell silent. The gunman robbed the cash register, grabbed the girl and headed for the door, just as Olan Chapman walked in.

The two men exchanged profanities.

The gunman let go of the struggling girl and swung the gun barrel at Chapman.

More profanities.

The gunman fired.

The blast propelled Olan Chapman back out the door, and opened a time frame for the bouncer to drop the gunman with a blackjack. When the police arrived: the gunman lay dead from a head concussion; the married men shielded their faces from TV cameras, and Olan Chapman had vanished.

"So, you were in a strip club, Olan !"

QUANTUM ROOTS II

"Ivy, the sign outside said gentlemen."

"You're full of bullshit, Olan, and I want your skinny ass home, and I mean now, and no more crap about being a wanted man. . .or .the cops won't need to kill you, because I will . ."

"Ivy, I have to go."

"Olan, don't hang up on me !"

"Ivy, I'm getting stomach cramps."

Olan Chapman turned off the talking phone. He took a wishful swig from the rum bottle, now empty. He staggered to the bathroom and fumbled for the light switch. He studied the ruffled hair, the whiskered face, the bloodshot eyes looking back from the mirror. He scowled. Then the weathered lines turned to a slight smile, as he removed the bullet proof vest, and thanked providence for military surplus stores.

Chapter 22

Two days later:

Alexis Grumman called her newly formed team together for an update in the vigilante case. Grumman's earlier team moved on to new assignments as vigilante sightings dried up. Now, with the recent film footage of Olan Chapman, Alexis was back in business with some fresh faces, a few former identities, and her youthful sidekick, Jeremy Wade.

"It's nice to be back on the east coast," said the junior agent trying to make eye contact with the lady general.

"Well, don't be liking it too much," said Alexis Grumman looking the other way, "Everybody here is heading west."

Does that include me, Alexis?

That includes you, Jeremy.

"Sounds like we have a breakthrough," said an agent wearing a confederate shirt and speaking with a southern drawl.

QUANTUM ROOTS II

"And you are?" asked Alexis.

"Agent Roberts, Ma'am, sniper."

"Roberts," said Alexis, mentally flipping through her data bank, "This is the second time we have had *Invisible Six* agents here. Would that be Zachery Roberts?"

"Yes, Ma'am."

"I thought you were assigned to Martin Swan."

"Colonel Swan is on honeymoon leave."

"Still?" queried Alexis.

"Yes Ma'am," replied Zach Roberts as laughter rippled through a dozen agents, who knew Swan had married a girl twenty years his junior, "Colonel Swan applied for an extension from what I understand."

"I see," said Alexis, "I hope you realize this is the DPA, Agent Roberts. We investigate and apprehend. We are not a commando unit. We do not feed live people to live alligators."

"It was just one person, Ma'am," countered Roberts, "And he was a terrorist."

Agent Zachery Roberts came from Martin Swan's *Invisible Six* Unit, whose escapades encircle the globe: blowing up bridges to thwart terrorists; trading gunfire with Colombian drug lords; rescuing fair maidens from kidnappers. But, the most recent assignment was the

Thanksgiving Day gunfight at Black Water crossing that became front page news.

The story goes that Cuban-aided terrorists tried to smuggle an explosive threat into Washington. The plan was to truck the cargo from Florida into Virginia. The terrorists would use the Suwanee River, a network of back roads, and a bridge encoded *The Black Water Crossing*. Luckily, details reached Martin Swan and the Invisible Six in time to stop the impending disaster, and capture two of the terrorists in the Okefenokee swamp.

Consequently, federal agents closed down the Washington, DC cell on information supplied by one of the captured terrorists. The second informant failed to testify due to a rare tropical disease known as Alligator Bite – at the hands of Zachery Roberts.

"He must have been terrified," said Alexis, dryly.

"He was," replied Zachery Roberts.

Alexis smacked a fiberglass pointer over a coffee tray, to stop laughter and restore order. She sipped cold water from a nearby cooler, and popped a candy mint. She called out to the invisible projectionist to bring up a map overlay. She said to the group, "We finally have something concrete to work with. A shopkeeper from Mt. Royal, NJ reports that person or persons unknown, broke into his computer outlet, and operated one of the additive manufacturing printers. The shopkeeper claims that an unknown amount of metal stock is missing, and that his chief technician found some .stl files in the system software."

"An additive manufacturing machine," bubbled Agent Reuben Goldberg, suddenly sitting up straight and addressing the floor, "That's a 3D printer."

"That is a 3D printer indeed," said Alexis, "So, now we know why we have no weapon reports,, bought or stolen. Chapman might have printed his own gun."

"Can he do that ?" asked Agent Spicer, back on loan from the CIA, "That would be an undertaking of unbelievable magnitude."

"Chapman is a computer wizard," reminded Alexis, "The man can make a micro chip sing *Dixie.* The .stl files found in the software were "build files" for a double action, Colt 45. Our best computer ace believes Chapman probably used a 3D technique called *Direct Metal Laser Sintering* to create a solid structure for the revolver parts. A carbon dioxide laser fires into a magnesium substrate to sinter powdered material into the finished product."

"The laser is a 200 watt Yb-fiber optic," chipped in Agent Goldberg, "The fused layers are typically 20 micrometers thick."

"Thank you for that, Reuben," said Alexis. Then addressing the group she said, "The shopkeeper found no .stl files for cartridges, so we have to believe that Chapman hasn't found a way to print bullets."

"And he won't," said a voice from the rear,

"And you are?" asked Alexis.

"Jocko Harrison," said agent James Harrison coming to parade rest, "Demolition rigger. If some--thing needs to be blown to bits, I'm your man. Large or small, makes no matter to me. I could plant a bomb in your cell phone."

"That's very comforting," said Alexis, "We have worked together before. . I believe it was two years ago at Niagara Falls ?"

"Yes, Ma'am."

"How many other members of Colonel Swan's unit are here?"

"Everyone but Joyner," said Harrison, "Josh was arrested for being drunk and disorderly. He goes on a binge every now and then."

"I see," said Alexis.

"Right now he's in the brig," said Harrison.

"Could we get back to making bullets?"

"Of course," replied Harrison, who went on to explain that a cartridge has four basic parts: the point;

the casing; the prime cap and the powder. Concluded Harrison, "The 3D laser could make the cartridge, but would blow the prime trying to produce a cap."

Alexis moved to the big screen. She traced the physical pointer over a zigzag pattern that covered all stops made by the vigilante. Each stop was marked with a computer circle, embedded on the overlay map. She conceded that no .stl files surfaced that would suggest bullet printing. However, software files did show up that would print money. Said Alexis, "I knew this zigzag pattern meant something beside idle roaming. Each *sighting* is near an outlet that contains a 3D printer, that can print a hat, boots, etc. They also stock printers that can print games, toys and paper products. From Salem NH to Scottsdale AZ, every stop was a waterhole for Chapman to refill his wallet."

"And money can buy bullets," mused Harrison, following Alexis' thought train.

"Small bills?" queried Agent Hendricks, on loan from the FBI.

"Probably Fives and Tens," replied Alexis, "Our latest data confirms that bogus twenties have largely outnumbered other counterfeit denominations. Thus, wary cashiers are less likely to check smaller bills."

Alexis, can we meet after this meeting?

Jeremy, I have a meeting with General Taylor, immediately following this meeting.

"So, where do we go from here, General?" said Agent Hendricks addressing the lady general.

Alexis ran the pointer tip west toward the Pacific Ocean, saying, "We know Chapman's in California. We have two leads, San Francisco and San Diego. One is north, the other south. I'm splitting up the team into two groups, Alpha and Bravo. Harrison will take Alpha Team south to San Diego. Hendricks will lead Bravo Team and cover Frisco."

"Are these leads reliable?" asked Agent Spicer on loan from the CIA.

"Very reliable," replied Alexis, "They came from Olan Chapman."

"Ma'am?"

"Chapman sent me a text," explained the lady general, "I think he savors this cat and mouse chase. Anyway, he sent us a message. *Catch him if we can.*"

"Brazen chap isn't he."

"Only when he's drinking," said Alexis, "Sober, Chapman could double as Mister Peepers."

"Ma'am, I find it scary that this Olan Chapman would have your cell phone number."

"So do I," agreed Alexis.

"Just how did that happen?" asked Spicer.

"We don't know," replied Alexis, "When we catch Chapman, we'll ask him."

"He must be an expect on hacking devices."

"Obviously, he's a level over our best internet technician," conceded Alexis with mouth drawn tight.

"So what's our work scope?" asked an agent.

"Stake out key outlets," replied Alexis, "Track down any recent 3D printer sales or rentals, This will take some legwork,gentlemen. It can't all be done on a computer. . . .yes Riggs ?"

"Do we have any hard evidence that Chapman uses a 3D printer?"

"Not yet," said the lady general, "We have forensic teams checking hair samples and fingerprints. Any other questions? . . . .yes Harrison?"

"Ma'am, it should be noted this vigilante does a fair job of mopping up bad guys."

"Harrison," replied Alexis after a long pause and a deep breath, "You're not the custodian who has to mop up the blood. This vigilante is not a heroic icon. Chapman is a loose cannon. . .and Harrison?"

"Yes, Ma'am ?"

"The Civil War is over, scrap the tee shirt, shave, get yourself some black oxfords and dress like a federal agent,"

"Yes Ma'am."

*   *   *   *   *

Sometime later, General James Ironhorse Taylor reminded Lt General Alexis Grumman that Colonel Martin Swan's men worked mostly undercover, and did not adhere to dress codes. Swan then came off honeymoon leave, to regroup the *Invisible Six* for a classified mission – including Agent James Jocko Harrison. After which, Alexis received six fresh agents to cover San Diego, San Juan County and the border between California and Mexico.

Part Three

KYLE   KEYES

Chapter 23

San Juan County

Hiram Cook was halfway through a handwritten shopping list, when trouble entered Bloomberry's sole grocery store.

Cook owned Cookies Fine Wines, located outside of town in San Juan County. Cook and daughter would show up on Main Street every Friday, to stock up with a week's worth of food supplies, and various other items. On this particular Friday, trouble showed up in the form of two motorcyclists named Spike and Ike Tabor.

Spike liked booze and women.

Ike liked women and booze.

Spike sported a Mohawk , designed to strike fear into the timid of heart. Ike wore a dirty ponytail held together with a rubber band. Both brothers looked like flea bags covered with tattoos, and each had a criminal history dating back to grade school. A second grade teacher caught Ike snatching handbags from the break room, while brother Spike raped a sixth grade teacher in an empty coat closet. Neither boy was sentenced due to being a minor.

"Did you see the ass on that," whispered Ike on their way to the cash register.

"I see'd," replied Spike eying up Hiram Cook's teenage daughter, Rebecca, "Maybe we oughta play a little grab ass."

Rebecca Cook was already full-bodied at sixteen. She had jet black hair that contrasted her dead white skin. Her speech ran slow, her dark eyes held that far away look, so common with autism. Sensing danger, the wary girl moved behind her father.

"Now don't be gitting scared," cackled Ike Tabor, who wore solid black leather with no markings. He slid dark goggles over a hairy head, and took phone pictures of the girl while saying, "We is only funning with you."

"Speak fer yourself," sneered Spike, "I intend to grab myself a handful of ass."

Grab ass was the latest teen craze sweeping the nation. Bands of hoodlums would race through retail markets, and grab sashaying posteriors whether the girl was alone or chaperoned. Spike and Ike figured if kids could do it, they could do it.

Hiram Cook issued several warnings to the two bikers, and then opened a cell phone. Hiram was not a fighter, nor a hunter. He was a deacon at the local church. He believed in God, and he believed in letting the authorities do their job. Spike responded by pulling a knife from his boot, before Hiram's cell phone could come to life.

"I just had this baby sharpened," said Spike as he ran a dirty finger over the clean blade, "Now, we is gonna prove that the sword is mightier than the phone, much mightier."

Laughing, brother Ike snatched Hiram Cook's cell phone, threw the flip-lid to the floor, and crushed the device with a boot heel. Ike then swung his own phone toward the girl and panted, "Why don't we pull her bra down and take a picture of those nice titties, whataya think, Spike?"

"I think you will pay for your sins," said Hiram.

"I'm in the cat bird seat," crowed Spike waving the knife, menacingly, "I'll decide what we do with the girl. We just might take her along with us."

"Settled," agreed Ike, "That ass will fit on my luggage carrier just fine."

"She rides with me," countered Spike, "I hold the trump card."

"Actually, I hold the trump card," warned Olan Chapman, coming around a grocery aisle. The slender computer wizard held up a cell phone and said, "I've already called 911 and the local authorities are on their way over."

Surprise is often the better sword. As all fell still, Abie Cohen returned from the back room to witness the tail end of the face-off, including the entrance of Olan Chapman. Cohen owned Abies Food Market and had tossed out Chapman earlier for shoplifting.

Olan Chapman drifted into Bloomberry because federal agents now watched computer outlets in all big cities from San Francisco to San Diego. Chapman was hungry, broke and had no resources to print his funny money. Cohen caught up with Chapman stuffing candy bars into deep pockets, and ushered the sheepish shop lifter out the market door with a harsh warning not to come back. He now re issued that warning.

"You heard the man," cried Spike, "Get your ass out of here while you still can !"

"He wasn't talking to me," lied Olan, "He was talking to you, mudder fucker."

And that started the melee. Spike charged Olan, who bounced a can of corn off the biker's chest. Ike ran to help his fallen brother, only to be tripped by Hiram Cook. Soon, the four men were hurling bottles, boxes and whatever wasn't nailed down. The free for all ended when Abie Cohen pulled a 32 from a counter drawer, and fired what was meant to be a warning shot.

Abie didn't like guns. He didn't like guns as an army recruit in Ft Dix, NJ. He got through basic training by paying the pit boss not to wave *Maggies Drawers*, every time he (Abie) missed the target. Now, clutching the weapon with two hands, he aimed the barrel toward the ceiling. He changed his mind. He didn't want to pay for a roof hole. He pointed the barrel toward the floor. He wiped sweat beads from a wrinkled forehead and fired. He missed the floor and hit Spike in the leg.

"I've been shot !" screamed the biker falling to the floor, "You stupid bastard, you shot me !"

"You shot Spike!" cried Ike.

"I'm going to bleed to death !" cried Spike.

"Spike is going to bleed to death," said Ike.

The wounded biker curled into a fetal position and grabbed his left leg. The bullet had entered behind the knee cap and took out cartilage. As fate would have it, Spike would eventually lose the leg and never ride again. Cried out Spike, "I need help now, I don't want to die !"

"We need help," pleaded Ike as Spike rolled around in agony, "Spike doesn't want to die."

"We need a tourniquet," said Olan Chapman.

"Yes yes," cried Abie Cohen, "A tourniquet."

"I don't think they use tourniquets anymore," said Rebecca in a soft, slow drawl.

"I need a belt," said Olan, "Somebody give me a belt !"

"Could we maybe move him outside?" asked Abie, "I just mopped this floor."

Olan Chapman used Ike's biker belt to cut off the blood streaming from Spike's leg wound. He tightened the belt loop just above the knee, ignoring the biker's painful howls. Slowly, the wound dried up as authorities showed up. Sirens sounded from all directions, as fire trucks, ambulances, police helicopters, and the highway patrol rolled in.

"Damn," moaned Abie, "They rolled everything. Now I vill get another fine."

"Abie, you won't get a fine," said Robbie Burke after bursting through the front door in response to the 911 call. Burke was local sheriff for Bloomberry Town--ship. The robust law officer had one squad car and two part time deputies, to patrol some sixteen square miles of California back country, east of San Diego and just north of Mexico. Border jumpers were common, as were cycle gangs who ran drugs and guns. Continued Sheriff Burke, "Abie, this not a false alarm. You get

QUANTUM ROOTS II

fined because you set off alarms when there's not a cloud in the sky. Now, I want everybody over in my office while I get this thing sorted out. "

"Who put the tourniquet on this guy ?" asked a first responder, while carrying Spike out on a stretcher. The ambulance, fire trucks and helicopter were all from Centerton, the county seat for San Juan County. The two motorcycle officers were highway patrolmen to backup Sheriff Burke. Additional county deputies were not on hand, due to internal resentment. At one time, Bloomberry was county seat. Then, as Centerton's population swelled to fifty thousand plus, the newly incorporated city took over as county seat, which left the Bloomberry sheriff with a political demotion and an obvious *authority issue.* Burke, who was as wide as he was tall, liked to make all decisions and give all orders, while grinding out a cigarette butt with a boot heel. Thus, this new scenario was more than a step down. It was also a blow to the little man's pride. Continued the first responder talking over Robbie Burke's loud voice, "We don't use tourniquets anymore !"

"That's what my daughter said," agreed Hiram, "Where are you taking him ?"

"County General."

"I hope it's a bumpy ride," said Hiram making

the sign of the cross.

"And who vill pay for this ambulance?" cried Abie Cohen, "I need a second mortgage now to pay for false alarms. If dispatch rolls everything one more time, I hit the five hundred dollar mark."

"Abie, get a dog to fetch the paper," said Sheriff Burke looking around, "The mutt won't set off your alarm at dawns early light, and where's the other guy?"

"What other guy," replied Hiram Cook, who had watched Olan Chapman slip quietly out the back door. Cook did not vote for Burke in past elections, and would not vote for Robbie Burke the next time around. And, Hiram was not about to blow the whistle on the man who had come to his rescue.

"I'm looking for the 911 caller who would not give me his name," said Burke counting noses, "He must be a stranger in town. I didn't recognize the voice."

"You must mean the shoplifter," replied Abie.

"What shoplifter?" asked Burke.

"The guy who put on that tourniquet."

Chapter 24

Cookies Fine Wines lie 15 miles from Bloomberry Township, and covered twenty acres of San Juan Valley. The blue ribbon winery was named Cookies in memory of Hiram Cook's wife, Marian who passed away giving birth to Rebecca Ann. The jovial thirty year old died some twenty four hours after delivery, from postpartum bleeding due to a botched Cesarean section. She left Hiram little cash, a large libel suit never settled, and a autistic daughter to raise.

"Rebecca isn't really retarded," explained Hiram Cook, "She suffers from mild Dyspraxia which causes motor slowness. Actually, Rebecca can be quite bright. She does my cash register work and has her own laptop computer. Course, I don't let her go online. Too much evil lurking up there in *The Cloud.*"

"Yes, clouds can be scary," said Olan greeting Hiram once inside the store entrance.

Hiram Cook chuckled. "I can see you don't know much about computers. . .what do you do for a living?"

"Odd jobs and swapping."

"Married?"

"Wife's back east," replied Olan twisting a gold band, third finger, left hand.

"Children?"

"No."

"How'd you find this place?" asked Hiram.

"I saw your *help wanted* ad in the paper."

"You walked fifteen miles?"

"I caught a ride part way," replied Olan looking around. The winery was an air conditioned, metal pre-fab that sat across from the main house, and next to a maintenance garage that housed farm tractors. A sign post welcomed buyers, wine tasters and anyone else wanting to take the hour long tour. A second sign said *No Smoking*. A third sign read: *Beware Of The Cat*. Olan shifted his backpack from shoulder blade to shoulder blade. Still sizing up the terrain he asked "Is that the vineyards across the road ?"

Hiram Cook nodded. "We grow more than grapes. We also grow oranges, strawberries, grape fruit, tomatoes," Cook paused to give Chapman a hard stare, "You being hunted ?"

"By my wife," said Olan.

"Touche," smiled Hiram Cook.

QUANTUM ROOTS II

"Who does all the picking?" asked Olan as two Latin Americans sauntered by..

"That's another *don't ask, don't tell*," said Cook.

"Touche," smiled Olan Chapman.

Blue solar panels stood everywhere to capitalize on Southern California's heavy sunlight. Cookies Fine Wines used solar to heat water, clean recycled bottles and run air conditioning. Consequently, a plaque award that read *Green Business Of The Year* hung over Cook's office desk. Corks, bottles and labels filled wall shelves. A wine vault occupied the back half of the building, where red and white wines were separated by type and age. The temperature controlled room served as the focal point for group tours. Up front, tables and chairs filled a tasting room where anyone of age could sample a wine of their choice.

"The wine tasting is a big drawing card for my business," said Hiram.

"I'm sure," said Olan.

"Customers can also buy wine at the register to take home," said Hiram, still sizing up Chapman, "Right now my new computer till is down, so I'm back to the old fashioned cash drawer. . .You disappeared after the sheriff showed. You sure you're not wanted ?"

"I'm sure," lied Olan.

"Abie Cohen mentioned something about you shoplifting," said Hiram.

"I was hungry," replied Olan.

"I won't put up with stealing," said Hiram.

"I won't steal from you," said Olan.

"And you keep your hands off Rebecca."

"I won't touch your daughter," replied Olan.

"Also, you don't drink my wine and you stay sober."

"I won't drink your wine, Sir."

Hiram Cook extended a hand. He agreed to give Olan room and board, plus minimum wage.

Olan smiled. Besides money and food, he was out of bullets and down to one burner. He didn't wish to be in this rural county that resembled a page from yesterday, but he had little choice. He sucked it up and reached for Hiram Cook's hand.

"You should have seen that biker's face when you nailed him with that can of corn," chuckled Hiram,

"And you should have seen that other biker's face, when you bounced that melon off his head," giggled Olan, "And where did you get that bag of horse shit?"

"That was cow manure," replied Hiram, "Abie stocks it for the local farmers."

QUANTUM ROOTS II

"Sure did stink."

"Yes it did,"   said Hiram Cook still brushing tiny particles off his flannel shirt,   "I won't do that again."

Chapter 25

The Black Hornets, motorcycle gang ran a giant sting business, true to it's name. The secretive, west coast club brought in mega bucks running contraband. And if federal law, enforcement agencies failed to close down their border crossing, the take would rise from mega bytes to terabytes, in computer language.

Riding with the Hornets was more than an honor, bigger than prestige. Peeling wheels with the Hornets garnered an annual mil per rider, and bike president, Carlton Milford Lansbury intended to add benefits to that package – namely health insurance, a goal that even he thought might be unattainable.

Carlton rose to club president the easy way. He shot the vice president in the back during a rival biker war. Later, he stood on the president's air hose, during a routine hospital visit. Once president, Carlton changed the club's image. No more ponytails. No beards. No pot. All bikes were equipped with stock mufflers. All bikers wore cycle helmets for safety – and to cover their Mohawk hair styles. Speeding was a no-no, and every club member carried proper ID to show any law enforcement they might encounter.

"We survive because we're outlaws inside the law," Carlton would stress to new members, "If you want to hum *Bad To The Bone*, or *Highway To Hell,* join another club."

Each bike carried two saddlebags for contraband. Cocaine connections were numerous in Colombia and Bolivia. The Black Hornets would bootleg the profitable goods north via a border tunnel that opened into San Juan County, just south of Bloomberry where Ike and Spike went missing.

"Who told the Tabors they could break file?" muttered Carlton referring to Ike and Spike.

"They pulled off at that general store," replied a biker known only as The Squirrel, "I moved up to fill in the gap.."

"What general store?" demanded Carlton.

"Abie's."

"Abie's !" cried Carlton, "That's back in San Juan County. Why wasn't I notified !"

"Sir, with all due respect," said a voice in a ring of faces, "You had your headset turned off."

The Black Hornets were camped out in a beach cove just north of San Diego. You could hear car horns to the east, lapping waves to the west. Their first buyer waited in L.A, next stop would be San Francisco. Then, it would be back to South America, which always included some detour such as Cancun, or Acapulco. These fun stops offset the tiresome trip north, which meant camping under the stars and guarding saddlebags.

"Spike flashed the beer sign," said the Squirrel, "And you know Ike's his shadow. . .they should have caught up with us by now, though."

Carlton Milford Lansbury swore softly. He could only blame himself for this sticky wicket. He didn't have his earphones tuned to biker calls. Instead, he chose to listen to a thumb drive loaded with Beethoven. Carlton also liked Bach, Mozart, and French cuisine food, rather than homeland based, beef and potatoes. His mother and father could trace their bloodlines back to Alfred The Great, first king of England, and one of Carlton's early cousins once played tennis for the amusement of Henry VIII. Carlton now turned to his first lieutenant and said, "I need a volunteer."

"You got one, Sir," said Edgar Caen jumping to his feet. The first lieutenant paused to wipe dust streaks from his polished black boots, then gave Carlton a fast salute. Caen was a tennis ace and also a wizard at lawn croquet. But his rise to first lieutenant hinged on two other factors: he always kissed the boss's ass, and he shot people just to watch them die.

"Not so fast," said Carlton catching the hungry gleam in Caen's beady eyes, "This is a fact finding trip. I want to know the where-a bouts of Spike and Ike, and I want a status report on their hooch."

"Yes, Sir."

"Are you gassed up ?"

"I will be, Sir."

Carlton pulled a hankerchief from his jacket. He turned his head to blow his nose. Allergies. He swore softly. San Diego climate was supposed to cure sneezes, hay fever, nasal problems from pillow feathers, lawn clippings and cat hair – or so he was told. He stared out at the choppy Pacific as he spoke to Caen, "You might encounter cell phone trouble getting out of San Juan County. I'll give you time to clear the mountains before you report in."

Rugged terrain and sparse cell towers hampered reliable communication in and out of San Juan County. There was just one cable carrier. Phone lines were in shoddy condition. Police radios used UHF, and farmers relied on citizens band. Consequently, Bloomberry held the feel of yesterday's world, running on today's calendar. Caen reported in at dinner time, the next day.

Cheeseburger bloated his stubby cheeks. A milkshake slurred his speech.

"What kind of trouble do we have," demanded Carlton Lansbury, "And stop sucking on that straw."

"Spike lost a leg," said Caen.

Carlton stared at his cell phone in disbelief. He stopped talking as a police helicopter hovered over -head. Then, as the chopper moved on, he received the fight details that led to the gunshot that took down Spike Tabor.

"Where is he now ?" asked Carlton.

"County General Hospital."

"And Ike ?"

"He's in the Bloomberry Jail for spitting on the local sheriff."

"Where's our payload?" asked Carlton.

"Still in the bike saddlebags."

"And the bikes ?"

"Impounded."

Carlton swore softly. Sooner or later, authorities would search the saddlebags, with or without a warrant. They would find the hooch. After which, they would grill the Tabor brothers, relentlessly. Carlton swore again,. He should have never let Ike and Spike into the club. They talked too much, and Carlton's bootlegging business depended on complete discretion. Club rules supported the utmost secrecy. No one rats out the club. No one turns state evidence, and no one takes a bribe to switch ships. Carlton drew a line in the sand with a forefinger. He asked, "How many Hornets believe we can trust Ike and Spike?"

Two hands went up.

"How many members think we can't."

Many hands went up.

"Settled," said Carlton to the group. Then, he asked into his phone, "You have your weapon?"

"Yes sir," replied Caen

"You know what to do," said Carlton, "And Caen ?"

"Yes sir?"

"Wait for darkness."

"Yes sir. . .and for your information, sir," said Caen, "There were three men against our two in that grocery store fracas."

"I'm listening," said Carlton.

"Beside the farmer and the store keeper," said Edgar Caen, "There was some drifter."

"I see," replied Carlton, "Okay . . get me the name and location of each man. We will avenge our fallen brothers."

KYLE KEYES

The biker called Squirrel now sat in the sand next to Carlton. He couldn't help but hear the conversation. He flicked a cigarette butt toward a small red bucket and said, "We need to keep face, sir. . .that's for sure."

"Yes," verified Carlton Lansbury, "And we will keep face. Many faces. It's almost Halloween."

"You have a plan ?" asked The Squirrel.

"I have a plan," replied Carlton Lansbury.

Chapter 26

Jeremy awoke to a ringing phone. He picked up the bedside handset and dropped the plastic receiver back onto the cradle. He closed an open window blind that overlooked the motel's swimming pool. He rolled over and pulled a fuzzy blanket over his head.

The phone rang again.

Muttering, he smashed a soft bed pillow over the harsh noise and turned a cold shoulder. The phone rang on. He swung bare feet onto chilly tile and covered his ears. His head hurt from too much cold beer the night before, his stomach churned from too much hot sauce. Still muttering, he grabbed the phone and said, "This is Room 105."

"This is the desk."

"I'll be skipping breakfast," said Jeremy.

"We don't serve breakfast," replied the phone.

"Do you have anything for a sour stomach?"

"I have a message for a Mister Wade."

"Speaking," replied Jeremy.

"You boss wants you to turn on your cell."

"I'd rather not," said Jeremy.

"Yes, she said you might say that."

Jeremy fumbled through the bed covers for his classified two-way. He did a quick closet search, came up dry, and then found the phone in one of his black oxfords. He hit the call icon for Alexis Grumman.

"Jeremy ?" queried the distant voice.

"Yes, General."

"I haven't been able to reach you, Jeremy."

"I've had my phone on the charger."

"Why don't I believe that," replied Alexis.

"You tell me," snapped Jeremy.

"You left town without so much as a goodbye."

"You were busy with the general, General."

"Why are you referring to me as General?"

"I'm sure you know why, General."

Silence.

"You heard," replied Alexis, finally, "Jeremy, I'm sorry."

"Stanley told me before I left."

"Stanley of course," said Alexis, "And did this informant tell you that your head was on the block if I didn't do something."

"No, he must have left that part out," said the junior agent, "He did mention that you went back for seconds and thirds and maybe fourths."

"And how would Stanley know that?"

"General Taylor's office light was still on when Stanley would come to work in the morning, and you would just be leaving the building,"

"I see," said Alexis Grumman, coolly, 'Very good detective work and now we need to get on with agency business."

"That's it !" exclaimed Jeremy.

"That's it."

"No further explanation?"

"Jeremy, it's better you hear this from me than some girl down the road, but size does matter," said Alexis, "And now moving on with business, we have two homicides in San Juan County."

"Alexis, that's hitting below the belt."

"Jeremy, I'm sorry."

"You're sorry ?"

"Jeremy, we need to talk about the homicides in San Juan County."

The victims were shot in the head with a hand gun. Caliber report was not in yet, nor was there any data on fingerprints or hairs samples.. Forensics runs a bit slow in San Juan County.

"Who were the victims ?" asked Jeremy, in a distant voice that smacked of disinterest.

"Two bikers," replied Alexis, "Local authorities found suspicious items in their saddlebags and called us."

"Contraband?" asked Jeremy.

"Pill bottles that look like aspirin."

"Opium?"

"Heroin," verified Alexis.

"The bad guys keep getting more clever," noted the junior agent.

"And it gets worse," said Alexis, "It appears we have a Mexican pill factory that's supplying a low key motorcycle gang with heroin disguised as baby aspirin."

"Baby aspirin?"

"Baby aspirin."

"Nothing's sacred anymore," muttered Jeremy.

"Jeremy, I'm sorry," replied Alexis, "Could we just let it go."

"So what do we have on this pill factory?"

"Very little," said the female director, "We can't be certain the source is even Mexico based. All we have are some clothing labels that read Mexico City. The pills could be manufactured farther south."

"And the cycle gang?" asked Jeremy.

"Again we have very little," replied Alexis, "And

evidently the club president – whoever that might be - wants to keep it that way."

Both shootings occurred between two and four-O-clock in the morning. An unknown gunman slipped into the unattended Bloomberry jail, and executed Ike Tabor. Later, an unknown gunman walked boldly into a County General Hospital room and put a bullet into Spike Tabor.

No one saw or heard anything.

"We think it was one gunman with a silencer," said Alexis, "There was no need for a security guard at that point in time. The contraband was found after the shootings."

"Doesn't sound like the vigilante," said Jeremy.

"It doesn't," agreed Alexis, "But Jim (General Taylor) wants it looked into."

"So now it's Jim?"

"Jeremy, for the last time, I'm sorry!"

*   *   *   *   *

Jeremy Wade rode on Route 5, just north of San Diego when the Black Hornets appeared in his rear view mirror. Systematically, the bikers split into two files and roared by Wade with no hoots or hollers. Cycle gangs certainly have changed, Jeremy would later ponder. This gang rode like police officers, quiet and orderly.

The bikers made the turn toward Bloomberry as one group, with Wade bringing up the rear. Then the uncanny happened. Jeremy's rocket boost ignited. The government issue, top secret, classified scooter took off like a shot. Wheels squealed. Running boards turned to small wings. Jeremy began throwing switches, but to no avail. The red and silver scooter went airborne. By the time Jeremy reached the front of the pack, the scooter was twenty foot in the air.

A small lake lay straight ahead. The road turned sharply southeast. A barbed wire fence ran between the road and the water. As the cycle gang made the turn in the road, the scooter flew over the fence and splashed into the water.

Chapter 27

Carlton Lansbury and Squirrel rode side by side at the head of the Black Hornets' motorcycle club. Both men looked up as Jeremy's scooter flew overhead, and dropped into the water.

"Holy hornet wings!" cried Squirrel.

"What the hell was that ?" asked Carlton.

"Maybe it was one of our new members," said Squirrel looking back to see a man swimming for his life."

Minutes later, Carlton pulled the club off the road to take a head count. The rest stop was a maze of soda machines, snacks and rest rooms. An entrance sign directed truckers and bikers to the rear lot. Asked Carlton while removing helmet, "Did you get a head count before the men scattered?"

"We are all here," replied Squirrel.

"Including our new members?"

"They need to get their bikes painted," said the Squirrel eyeballing two red cycles squeezed between an array of black and gold wheels. All Hornet bikes were black with gold fenders that bore small paint blotches, designed to resemble bees. Some members had hornet patches sewn into their saddlebags, as well.

"There will be time for bike painting later," said Carlton "Right now the mission comes first."

"Where did these new guys come from?" asked the Squirrel

Carlton Lansbury used a black leather glove to wipe dew off a concrete picnic bench. He eased down gingerly, and opened his cell phone's notebook. Carlton kept a backlog of applicants seeking club membership. Now with Ike and Spike gone, his foresight was paying off. Said Carlton, "Deek with no last name listed, hails from South Carolina where he made a career of robbing Piggly Wiggly stores. Cooter – he's the one with the fur lined helmet – came down from Alaska. He claims to be bike riding since age two, and under occupation, he has *Bail Jumping.* "

"We must be desperate," said Squirrel.

"We need to be back at full strength going into this mission," said Carlton, "And when I made the calls, these two men were nearby and available. ..what do you have on that flying bike?"

The Squirrel powered down his smart phone and caught a yellow snack bag coming his way from fellow biker, Odgen Cooper. More Hornets filtered back from concession machines as Squirrel cried, "Don't think you are buying me off Coop. I get the farmer's daughter next after Caen."

"We get a farmer's daughter?" asked new rider, Deek with no last name.

Ike Tabor's phone pictures of Rebecca Cook went to The Squirrel first via social media, and then made the rounds, as each club member fantasized what he would do with the busty teenager. Somewhere amid the *likes*, *dislikes* and *remarks,* someone dubbed her *The Farmers Daughter.*

"She will go good with some beer," suggested Cooter.

"We get the beer in Mexico," said Carlton to the new member, "We try and keep a low profile here in the states, and I will make the decision on the girl. Now, can we get back to the flying bike !"

Squirrel polished off the chips, wadded up the empty bag, caught a warning look from Lansbury and walked the crumpled wrapper to the trash can. Other bikers followed suit. Said the Squirrel now back at the table, "Carlton, there's no word on the street about a flying bike. No word on social media. Nothing. Nada."

"Must be top secret," mused Carlton.

"Probably government issue," said Squirrel.

"Could be some kind of spy craft," said Carlton.

"I wonder why it fell in the water?"

"It doesn't matter," said Carlton, "The point is that we are being watched."

'So we throw in the towel?" asked Squirrel.

Carlton arose from the stolid picnic table, slowly, thoughtfully. He stared at the distant mountain range that divided San Juan County from San Diego. Finally, he said, "We are too close to the border to scrub the mission. . .I have a plan to slow down the feds and soften up our target. We are going to knock out their communication."

Chapter 28

"Who owns the forty-five?" called down Olan Chapman from the garage loft.

"Forty-five?" Rebecca called back up in the form of a question.

"The pistol," said Olan, "There's an army issue 45 caliber, up here."

"Oh. . the gun," replied the girl, "That belongs to my Uncle Frank."

The pull-down steps connected the garage floor to the overhead loft, which was now Olan Chapman's new home. A brown cot ran below a double sash window that overlooked acres of vineyard. Two clothes chests held an assortment of shirts, tees and socks. A portable closet made from brown cardboard, held trousers. The bath was a small washroom on the ground floor, with nothing but a stained sink and leaky commode. Oddly enough, the door locked from both sides. Occasionally, when on a solo errand, Hiram would use the double lock to keep Rebecca from wandering away.

KYLE KEYES

The garage bedroom was first furnished for Hiram's twin brother, who had a problem staying on the wagon. Frank and Hiram were not identical twins, but parental - as was their character. Hiram was the proverbial tea toddler, while Frank would get smashed at least twice a year. After which, wife Edie would start throwing things, and Frank would wind up in Hiram's garage bedroom.

"Uncle Frank's not allowed to visit anymore," said Rebecca in monotones, "Except to come back and pick up his belongings."

"How's that ?" called down Olan.

"Uncle Frank put his finger up my vagina."

"Oh," said Olan caught flatfooted..

It happened on a steamy July night. Rebecca had turned sixteen, Uncle Frank was half in the bag. Hiram shut down the grille and disappeared for a short nap. Rebecca pulled her bikini clad body out of the backyard pool, when her uncle lured her into the garage.

"He had a birthday surprise for me," said the teenage girl, "Now I'm not permitted in the loft any--more."

Rebecca was first up the ladder with Uncle Frank in tow. The girl just reached the top when Frank pulled the string on her bra. He reached around her bare body, still wet from pool water, and grabbed her bobbing breasts. Rebecca screamed. Uncle Frank groaned with mounting pleasure. He yanked her skimpy, swim suit down, and thrust a finger between her legs. Rebecca screamed, again. Frank had wanted to ravish Rebecca on the bedroom cot. Now, he changed plans and decided to take her right there on the ladder steps. He just got his penis in hand, when brother Hiram burst through the side door, in response to Rebecca's screams. The two brothers exchanged looks, profanities and then fists, as they often did in a time long gone by. Their parents claimed the twins would fight over a gum drop.

"This sounds bigger than a gumdrop issue," said Olan listening to Rebecca's tale of black eyes and bloody noses, "Are there any bullets for this gun ?"

"I don't know what got into Uncle Frank," said Rebecca, "Daddy says it was the Devil."

"It wasn't Prince Charming," said Olan rooting through drawers, nooks and crannies, "There should be bullets somewhere near a gun."

The girl stood at the ladder base and continued to stare at the shadowy movements above. Now, out of the pool, the evening air felt cool. She pulled the towel off her wet hair, and wrapped her shoulders. She looked about the garage. Hiram Cook invoked a safety rule for weapons and ammunition. He never kept a gun and it's bullets in the same place. Rebecca's dark eyes rolled over a weathered work bench when a sudden light bulb lit.

"I remember," she called up the steps.

Olan stopped rummaging through old uniforms and service medals. He grabbed a two by six and swung down the steps. The bullets half filled a cartridge box, buried behind some tools, in the bottom drawer of the workbench.

"Daddy keeps these hidden," said the girl, "He doesn't like guns."

"Neither do I," said Olan Chapman.

"Can you drive a car?" asked Rebecca.

"I have a license," replied Olan.

"I often wish for a drivers license," said Rebecca staring wistfully at the family station wagon parked toward the rear of the garage. The stick shift vehicle was more than transportation, it was also Hiram Cook's idle hour hobby. Hiram kept the heavy steel relic, whistle clean, serviced and booted with new rubber. A roof rack carried luggage when needed. The rear seat folded down to haul groceries back from town. "Papa calls the wagon Ole Ironsides."

QUANTUM ROOTS II

"I think the car qualifies for antique tags," said Olan giving the station wagon a passing glance before returning his attention to the cartridge box.

"Papa wants to thank you for fixing our cash register," said the girl, "He has a friend who said it couldn't be repaired and that we would have to buy a new one."

"We all have our little talents," said Olan," Mine is computers."

"I have a computer," said Rebecca.

"Yes," replied Olan who had seen the desktop hard drive, setup for video games only, "I noticed it doesn't go online."

"Papa won't let me online," said the girl toying with a blond curl that dangled down her forehead and covered one eye, "Papa says it's nothing but smoke and mirrors."

"I'm sure father knows best," smiled Olan.

Chapter 29

"You're strapping the dynamite to the wrong legs, Coop."

Odgen Cooper ignored criticism coming from Carlton Lansbury and continued wiring six explosive sticks to the cell tower support. T'was not an easy job for a bloke with three fingers missing on one hand and no thumb on the other – the result of childhood play-time with firecrackers. Wire snips lay nearby. Shredded security fence littered the sandy soil that surrounded the cell tower base. Most Back Hornet members stayed roadside, some 'hundred foot away.

"Carlton, we don't need to drop the tower," called out Bernard Sytes, also known as The Mouse.

"How's that?" queried Lansbury.

"All we need do is disconnect the digital signal processors."

Primary and electrical power sheds surrounded the base station, along with a weathered structure that held the GSM systems. Called back Carlton Lansbury,

"And just where might these digital signal processors

be found?"

"I'm Googling it," replied The Mouse twitching a tiny mustache beneath a tiny nose.

"And?"

"It's searching."

"I'm waiting, Mouse."

"My phone battery just died."

"Blow the tower," snapped Carlton Lansbury talking to Odgen Cooper.

Not all terrorists are eastern camel jockeys. Some are home grown. The cell tower fell across the road that connects San Diego with Bloomberry. Bikers flew in all directions. The explosion could be heard as far south as Cancun, Mexico.

"Dammit Mouse," screamed Lansbury, "It fell the wrong way."

"It blocked the road," pointed out Bytes siding with Odgen Cooper.

"We don't want the road blocked," spit Carlton Lansbury, "We don't want to tip our hand."

"So now what?" queried The Squirrel.

"We move plans up a day," decided Lansbury staring at a gap through the mountains, "We settle up with that store keeper that shot Spike. Then we track down that grape farmer and his hired hand."

KYLE KEYES

"And what about the girl?" asked Bytes.

"The girl will bring top money in Mexico City," said Carlton, "And if she's a virgin, the opening bid will start even higher."

"Caen isn't gonna like this," said Cooper.

"Edgar will follow orders," snapped Carlton.

Chapter 30

The Hornets rolled into Bloomberry with little noise and no fanfare. Still, you could feel the heat come off the street, as engines shut down and boot heels hit black macadam. Edgar Caen waited by a fire plug and a dented sign that read *No Parking*. Traffic was light, and shopping at a standstill. Said Caen, "Computers are down, along with my cell phone."

"We had to drop the tower ahead of schedule," explained Carlton Lansbury.

"Complications?" asked Caen.

"We might be under federal surveillance," said Lansbury who went on to describe the hi-tech cycle that flew overhead and crashed into the water, "Only the government would have that technology."

'A flying bike," grunted Edgar Caen, "Sounds like a death toll for easy riders, everywhere."

"There is an upside," pointed out Lansbury, "With the tower down, we now have our soft target."

Caen touched a match to a cigarette and blew a smoke ring at a poster nailed to a phone pole. The sign read: *Worldwide Peace Movement, Let It Begin With Bloomberry.* Smiling, he said, "The target is softer than you know."

"How's that?" queried Carlton.

"The town ran a *gun buyback* just last week," replied Edgar Caen, "Some ladies bunch was behind it. Probably wanted to git their mugs on the tube."

"People turned in their weapons?"

"To the last gun."

"By jove," said Carlton Lansbury. Then nodding toward the sheriff's office, "Is he alone?"

"His deputy is with him," replied Caen

"And the store keeper?"

"He lives over top of the market."

"Is he alone ?" asked Carlton.

"Yes, Sir."

"Good," replied Carlton nodding to Caen, "You take the men and silence the law. Coop and I will round up the shop keeper."

"I thought tomorrow was D day," said Caen.

"We are moving now," snapped Lansbury who resented being questioned, "Just follow orders."

Abie Cohen was a clutter-bug. Clutter filled the grocery aisles. Clutter covered counter tops, and clutter led the way up the side steps to Cohen's meager living quarters. Odgen Cooper tripped over some shredded tax records, while Carlton Lansbury used a cell phone to light the creaky steps.

"Sorry," whispered Cooper.

"So much for the element of surprise," sighed Lansbury.

More darkness waited upstairs. Carlton fumbled for a switch and suddenly there was light. They were in the kitchen. The two men then went on a room to room search for Abie Cohen. Cooper found the balding shop keeper huddled behind hanging clothes in a bedroom closet.

"Pull him out," ordered Carlton.

"It was an accident," moaned Abie squinting into Carlton's pen light, "I didn't mean to kill one of your bikers."

"You didn't kill the biker," said Carlton.

"Ah, that is good," said Abie.

"We had to kill the biker," said Carlton.

"I am sorry," said Abie, "I am so sorry."

"We need to send out a message," said Carlton, "I want the world to see what happens when you attack a black hornet. And we need your help."

"Yes yes," cried Abie, "I vill do anything."

"I'm happy to hear that," said Carlton, "We've

heard your tale, now we will listen to your squeal."

Meanwhile outside, Edgar Caen and the other Hornets swarmed the sheriff's office as a hive of many who were now one. They found Sheriff Robbie Burke with feet propped on a giant maple desk, cowboy hat covering face and one over-sized mustache. He jumped upward only to be quickly subdued amid a burst of questions mixed with angry profanities. Deputy Otis Freebe appeared from a small wash room in time to be hand cuffed to his boss. Burke's other deputy was away on a fishing trip.

"What's going on?" cried Freebe.

"We are shooting a Halloween movie," cackled a gang member behind a rubber warlock mask, "And you two have lead roles."

"Shut up," barked Edgar Caen.

"Yes sir," replied the warlock mask.

Edgar Caen surveyed the two room facility. Bars covered all windows. Various plaques adorned the side walls. A rifle rack held hunting weapons and a shot gun. Two confinement cells sat empty in the back room, and a slat wood crate overflowed with handguns turned in by residents who no longer wanted to bear arms.

"We could lock them up right here in their own jail," suggested Bernard Sytes from behind the rubber mouse mask.

"No," snapped Caen, "We follow the plan."

"But Edgar," muttered The Mouse, "We are not terrorists."

"We follow the plan," repeated Caen.

Outside, excitement filled the street as a giant bull horn explained to a swelling crowd that the Black Hornets were fiming a Halloween movie. The film would be titled Nightmare On Main Street, and would star the shop keeper, Abie Cohen, Sheriff Robbie Burke and Deputy Sheriff, Otis Freebe. Residents would act as the supporting cast and perform as frightened onlookers.

"I don't see any cameras," called out a voice from the crowd.

"We are using phone cameras," replied the bull horn, "This is a social media film."

"Then I assume we don't get paid," chided the faceless voice, bringing a burst of laughter, followed by growing curiosity and light chatter.

The festive mood ended abruptly. Shortly after the Hornets pushed Burke and Freebe from the sheriff's office, into the street, a body flew out the second story window of Abie's general store.

The body was bare, tape bound and blindfolded. A rope noose wrapped the neck, with the far end tied to an iron radiator inside the window. The body came down head first, then did a quick U-turn at rope's end.

Those close by heard Abie Cohen's neck snap.

"Are you bikers crazy!" screamed Burke, "You guys are nuts. Somebody call the county !"

"Everybody stay put !" ordered Lansbury with handgun drawn, "I don't want you good folks to miss the film finale. This is the stuff that earns an Oscar."

"You freaking bikers!" spit Robbie Burke, "You think you are above the law."

"Your phone lines are down," reminded Carlton Lansbury, "You have no guns. I think that makes me the law."

"You are crazy!" cried Burke over and over, "You freaking bikers are crazy."

"Crazy?" laughed Carlton Lansbury giving his first lieutenant the high sign, "You want crazy?"

Suddenly, Edgar Caen emptied his weapon into the dead body of Abie Cohen. Blood shot out like a series of tiny volcanoes. Screams filled the mid-day air. Town folks scattered to nooks and crannies, only to find their cell phones were dead. Caen then pushed the sheriff and deputy to their knees and held the gun to their heads..

"Carlton, don't do this," pleaded Bernard Sytes.

QUANTUM ROOTS II

"We are not terrorists. I don't want people calling me a towel-headed, Muslim."

Slowly, Lansbury reached for Caen's gun, saying, "The mouse is right, Edgar. We are not camel jockeys. Besides, I have a better idea."

An hour later, Carlton Lansbury mounted up and led the Black Hornets out of Bloomsbury. He peered back at the three men hanging from a second story porch railing. Their dangling feet almost touched the bloody Main Street macadam. The Hornets had hung Sheriff Burke, Abie Cohen and Otis Freebe, side by side, despite public protest.

"That was a nice touch," shouted Edgar Caen over cycle noise.

"I thought it was," replied Carlton Lansbury.

The Hornets had hung the Jew in the middle.

Chapter 31

Hiram Cook signed off his citizens band radio with a series of threes and eights, then snapped off the desktop receiver and ran down the steps to find Olan and Rebecca finishing up a late lunch. Hiram stopped abruptly at the table head, and ran a troubled hand through what was left of his once untamed hair.

"What's up?" asked Olan.

"I just got off the two-way with Henry down the road."

"And?"

Hiram Cook stared at his autistic daughter. His facial frown deepened. He slapped his pockets for a wallet that wasn't there, and then sent the girl upstairs on a fool's errand. After which, he relayed to Olan Chapman the gruesome details of the Black Hornets assault on Bloombury.

"Sounds like they held everybody hostage," muttered Olan, "What happened to the land lines?"

"Henry thinks the biker gang blew up some key transformers."

QUANTUM ROOTS II

"Where are they, now?" asked Olan referring to the bikers.

"Heading this way," replied Hiram.

"What do they want?"

"Revenge."

Chapter 32

Henry Wiley stood on his farmhouse porch when the Black Hornets roared down his mile long driveway. Wiley didn't like trespassers, and he liked motorcycles, even less. He spit a stream of tobacco juice toward a sign that read *Private Property* and said, "I guess you fellows can't read."

"We are looking for Hiram Cook," said Carlton Lansbury.

"Well, you won't find him here," said Wiley.

Edgar Caen had braked next to Lansbury. The two men swapped looks. Carlton Lansbury nodded. Caen pulled a gun and aimed the barrel right at Wiley's head. After which, Wiley stopped snapping the straps on his bib overalls, and pointed a nervous finger, east.

"How far?" asked Lansbury.

"Three maybe four miles," said Wiley.

"Thank you for helping," said the Black Hornet leader, "You have a phone?"

"It's out of service."

"Is that a CB antennae on the roof?"

QUANTUM ROOTS II

"It is," said Wiley.

"Does it send and receive messages?"

"It does," said Wiley.

"Shoot him," said Carlton Lansbury turning to Edgar Caen, "Mark it down as collateral damage."

Chapter 33

Olan Chapman left the table, no longer hungry. He stared out the picture window at a cocky rooster chasing down a noisy hen. His knees felt a bit watery, his stomach queasy. He swung his gaze from the driveway to the garage. His magic attire was in the overhead loft. He needed to get to that backpack.

"I want you to take the keys to the wagon and get my daughter out of here," said Hiram grabbing a rifle from over the fireplace, "Take the back road out and don't stop til you get to the county seat."

"I don't drive," said Olan.

"I think you do," said Hiram.

"We could all go," suggested Olan.

"They'll catch us within five miles," said Hiram, "Somebody needs to stay here and buy time, and I'm the land owner."

"What's going on, Papa," asked Rebecca, half way down the stairs.

"You and Olan are going on an errand," said Hiram.

"Why do you have the gun down, Papa ?"

QUANTUM ROOTS II

"I'll stay here," said Olan, "You take Rebecca and be off."

Hiram rested the rifle across a glass top coffee table. The bullets were hidden in an upstairs closet. He stared at Olan Chapman intently as he asked, "You know how to load this thing ?"

"I can learn," replied Chapman.

"That's what I thought," said Hiram.

"What's going on, Papa ?" asked Rebecca.

"You are going with Mr Olan," replied Hiram handing over the car keys, "You and Mr Olan are going on an errand."

Olan Chapman frowned. He knew that Hiram couldn't take out the entire biker gang, At best, he could maybe start some blood shed that would slow down search and seizure proceedings, but it would only be a small window for getaway time. The bikers would soon realize Hiram was alone, and then kill the wine maker before tracking down his daughter. The frown on Chapman's face began turning angry. His eyes started to change. His queasy knees steadied. He grabbed Rebecca's hand and headed for the station wagon.

The outside garage lie some 'hundred foot from the house. Rebecca stopped midway between the two buildings. She looked back. Her blue eyes went from question marks to suspicion as she said, "I know there is something wrong."

"Rebecca, we need to hurry," said Olan masking concern with an even voice.

"But, why does papa have the gun down?"

"Probably wants to clean the weapon," lied Olan.

The Black Hornets were just minutes away. Olan's mind raced. He needed to get the girl out of sight. His gear was in the back of the overhead loft. The wagon would require an ignition override. He flipped open his two-way and checked satellite strength. He tapped *search*. He typed in *solenoid* and *clock timer*. Then, he grabbed Rebecca Cook's arm, and pulled the resisting girl into the garage.

Chapter 34

Hiram finished loading the Thirty Ought Six as he realized the station wagon never left the garage - or he had failed to hear the vehicle leave, which was not likely with that hole in the muffler. He hustled down the steps, rifle in hand, and burst onto the front porch.

The double doors to the garage stood closed

"Damn," he murmured.

Providence requires timing, and precision timing lies beyond human comprehension. Hiram was about to leave the porch and head for the garage, when he heard the cycles. He froze behind the porch railing as Black Hornets filled his driveway. Some made a circle before stopping. Others fired guns into the air like a bunch of yahoo cowboys. A wayward bullet was later found in that porch railing.

"Where is he?" demanded Carlton Lansbury raising the black shield that covered his face.

"Who you looking for?" yelled Hiram.

"Your hired hand," replied Carlton, "Word has it that he took part in the shooting of Spike Tabor."

"Word has it wrong," said Hiram.

"I don't think so," replied Carlton.

"He's not here," said Hiram.

"I think he is," replied Carlton.

"I let him go earlier this week," said Hiram.

Carlton Lansbury stared at Hiram Cook. The two men locked eyes for a long moment before Lansbury said, "I think you are lying."

"And I think you are on my property," warned Hiram Cook.

By now all cycles had stopped. Guns were silent. Edgar Caen leaned over and muttered to Carlton Lansbury, "Sir, he's fucking with us."

Carlton nodded his agreement. The bikers were growing restless. It was time to end pointless patter. Time to call out his adversary. He turned to Edgar Caen and said, "You're up, Bulldog."

Edgar Caen sat with feet spread, legs open to keep the bike upright. He pulled off the rubber doggie mask and shook his shaven head. Grinning, he grabbed his testicles and called out, "Here's the deal old man. You turn the hired hand over to us now, and we go easy on your daughter."

Hoots and hollers filled the late afternoon air.

"And," continued Edgar Caen, "We let you die

a quick death."

Hiram Cook swore softly and swung the rifle barrel over the porch railing and toward the biker gang. Laughing stopped first. Then, all activity stopped as a hidden car engine roared into life.

"He's in the garage !" yelled Carlton.

The warning came too late. Old Ironsides burst out the double doors like a giant steel ball shot from a cannon. The garage shook as rusty hinges popped. Rubber squealed. Muffler roared. The bikers never had a chance to react. Bodies flew in all directions as the station wagon crashed into the Black Hornets and came to rest on top of two cycles, pinning the riders under the drive shaft.

Screams pierced the air.

Bikers scrambled to regain their feet,

Suddenly, a figure appeared in the open garage doorway.

"Carlton, who the hell is that !" cried Bernard Sytes.

Lansbury lay pinned beneath his bike, his fallen headset playing Mozart's rendition of Halleluiah. He twisted to eyeball the silhouette framed in the open doorway. The shadowy figure wore a flat top stetson, a U.S. Marshall's badge and a low slung gun belt. A gusty floor draft blew dust balls around his black boots. He looked like a page from a Civil War book.

"Who the hell is he?" mumbled Odgen Cooper.

"It's that vigilante guy," cried a biker who read newspapers and wore a rubber mask that looked like a duck, "He's wanted for murder one."

"What's he doing here?"

"Just shoot him !" commanded Lansbury, "We don't care who he is, just shoot him !"

Bernard Sytes was first to come up with a hand gun. The jittery biker rolled free of his fellow bikers to get an open shot. The vigilante slapped leather and Sytes took a bullet through the head. More shots followed. More bikers fell. The vigilante reloaded.

"Somebody shoot that sonofabitch !" screamed Carlton Lansbury

The vigilante took out Lansbury and Caen, last. Edgar Caen came close to snatching the Luger from his saddlebag, when a head shot went up his nose, blew out his eyes, and lodged in his safety helmet. Carlton Lansbury died, still pinned under his cycle. A final vigilante bullet silenced the music, as though the head set was the enemy.

Now, more screams.

The two bikers trapped under the station wagon

still lived. Hiram Cook stepped clear of the porch railing and swung the rifle barrel toward the station wagon as he muttered, "So, you bastards wanted to fuck with my daughter."

Hiram knew where the gas tank was located. He fired once and the rear end of the wagon exploded into a giant fireball, painting red and yellow flames against a backdrop of distant hills. He made the sign of the cross, then ran in the direction of his daughter's screams. He hurried past the vigilante and found Rebecca locked in the garage bathroom. He undid the outside lock, and for many long minutes, father and daughter embraced.

When they exited the garage, the vigilante was gone.

Chapter 35

Darkness and the big whirlybird arrived together. Agent Jeremy Wade guided the federal chopper down with a lantern borrowed from Hiram Cook. Landing became difficult due to sudden wind gusts, forcing the pilot to touch down next to the burned out station wagon. Called out Wade as Alexis exited beneath the whirling chopper blades, "Try to avoid the mud mixed with blood."

"Thank you for that, Jeremy," called back the director for the Department of Paranormal Activities.

"You missed the clean up," said Jeremy.

County Fire And Rescue had just cleared out. Old Ironsides had been up-ended briefly, a tactical move needed to remove two badly charred bodies. There was no tow truck available. Thus, a group of first responders with cowhide gloves, rolled the wagon over so remains could be put into body bags. The same responders rolled the vehicle back to an upright position to satisfy Hiram. Earlier, the other bikers and their cycles were carted off in a giant box truck.

QUANTUM ROOTS II

"I can't tell you anything I haven't told everyone else," said Hiram Cook while introducing his daughter to Alexis Grumman, "Feel free to look around, and just call me Hiram. I don't go by Mister Cook."

"Of course," said Alexis, "I know this has been a long day, so I'll keep it brief."

Long day was an understatement to be sure. Moments after Hiram Cook's SOS hit the CB circuit, the world descended on Cookies Fine Wines like buzzards swarming over road kill. County mounties showed up first, followed by the California Highway Patrol, state police, F.B.I., the news media, firetrucks and one ambulance. After which, San Juan County Sheriff, Ben Henderson radioed Centerton headquarters to send out the box truck.

This is not your typical vigilante shooting, an eager news person told the world via satellite. *This is a massacre.*

"I need to see Chapman's sleeping quarters," said Alexis as the foursome walked toward the house.

"I don't know any Chapman," said Hiram.

"Olan Chapman was your hired hand."

Hiram Cook immediately changed direction and headed for the garage, explaining that he knew Olan Chapman as Olan Jacobs. Hiram went on to describe

Jacobs as mild mannered, soft spoken and gentle. Concluded Hiram as they entered the garage, "This vigilante is a killer. He shot those bikers like guppies in a fish bowl. Jacobs on the other hand can't even load a gun, which is why I chose to stay behind."

"This is the door that locks from the outside?" queried Alexis stopping by the wash room.

"Yes ma'am."

"According to this fax," said Alexis tapping a folded sheet of yellow paper, "You found your daughter locked in here after the shooting ended."

"Olan was supposed to drive Rebecca to the county seat," said Hiram.

"So why didn't he?" asked Alexis.

"I was crying," explained Rebecca looking from her father to the female general, "Papa took down our hunting rifle. Papa never takes down our hunting rifle unless something is wrong."

Alexis had Rebecca sit on a milking stool. Then the director for paranormal activities, softly said to the girl, "Rebecca, I want you to think real hard and try to remember exactly what Mister Olan said."

"I can remember what Mister Olan said."

"I know you can," replied Alexis.

"Mister Olan said to stay out of sight. He said

no harm was going to befall us. Mister Olan said he knew some one who could help."

"Boy, did he ever," murmured Hiram, "Where the hell did that guy come from ?"

"Alexis, we need to talk," said Jeremy in deep whispers meant for the lady general's ears only.

"Agent Wade, nothing has changed since our last little talk," said Alexis Grumman while fingering a knot hole in the wash room door. The small round hole was approximately three foot off the floor, and provided an open view to the ladder steps that led to the loft. Said Alexis to Rebecca, "You must have seen someone go up the steps."

"I saw Mister Olan go up into the loft," replied Rebecca.

"And who did you see come down?"

"A stranger came down," said Rebecca,

Alexis opened her classified phone. She scanned through the gallery and stopped on a photograph of the vigilante.

"That's him," said Rebecca.

"Actually, something has changed," whispered Jeremy to Alexis, "And we really do need to talk."

"We're on the clock," snapped Alexis to Jeremy Wade. Then turning to Hiram Cook, she said, "I need to poke around your loft. I can get a warrant."

"No need," said Hiram Cook, "No one else got one."

Alexis and Jeremy climbed the rickety steps while Hiram and the girl stayed downstairs. Ten minutes of looking through drawers and shoe boxes, turned up nothing and they started back down.

"For what's it's worth," said Jeremy, "Molly and I are going on a cruise when this mission is over."

"Molly from Nickles Bar & Grille?"

"The same."

"Molly with the big boobs?"

"Alexis, tit size does matter."

"That's hitting below the belt, Jeremy," snapped Alexis, "And for what it's worth, only a bimbo would put a tattoo of a tit on a tit."

'I think you're jealous," said Jeremy.

"I'm not jealous and don't call me, Alexis."

"I see you still wear pink panties," said Jeremy as Alexis followed him down the ladder.

"Jeremy, little pitchers are listening!"

"Can we talk later?"

"I'll think about it, Agent Wade."

"So, what were we looking for?" asked Jeremy.

"We were looking for a 3D printer."

"Well, there wasn't any."

"I saw that," admitted Alexis.

"I did find this," said Jeremy holding out a coin on a string.

"Looks like a coin on a string," said Alexis.

"It's a silver dollar with a hole through it," said Jeremy Wade holding the coin up to the light, "Can't read the date. . .the markings are worn off."

"Interesting," said Alexis, "But we're looking for additional evidence that will verify how Olan Chapman becomes the vigilante."

"I wanted it to be a worm hole," said Jeremy dropping the silver dollar in his pocket, "If only we had some hard evidence."

"Worm holes sound like science fiction to me," said Hiram Cook hitting the light switch and taking Rebecca by the hand, "I don't let my little girl watch that scary stuff."

"I'm . .almost . .seventeen," said Rebecca.

I don't like scary stuff either," said Alexis "Just one more question and we're out of here. . .Who drove the car out of the garage ?"

Hiram Cook led the way outside to the badly charred station wagon. A crowbar wedged between the dashboard and the gas pedal. The vehicle was still in gear, the ignition key turned on. Hiram lifted the hood and pointed to a small black box mounted to the firewall, next to the starter solenoid. Explained Hiram, "This is an Inverter. It converts DC current to AC current. It came from inside the wagon. I used it to heat coffee. The clock next to it is a converter for my DC outdoor lights. I kept it with the holiday stuff back in the garage. The inverter is wired from the battery to the AC portion of the timer. When the clock timed out, the bottom contacts sent DC to the starter solenoid."

"Damn," whistled Alexis, "It bypassed the starter switch."

"Your assistant here helped me figure it out."

"And we found something else," said Jeremy Wade swelling with importance, "Hiram's can of starter fluid is empty."

"The whole gallon is missing," said Hiram, "I think it was emptied into the gas tank, and that would explain why ole Ironsides hit that door doing ninety-four. What it doesn't tell us is who rigged this up ."

"Olan Chapman," said Alexis.

"My handyman?"

"The same."

"I never would have guessed," mused a stone -faced Hiram, "I stumbled across his computer skills, but he doesn't strike me as a mechanic."

"Well, we know your daughter didn't rig the station wagon," said Alexis, "She was locked up in the bathroom. . . .is that your CB antennae up on the house roof?"

"That's her," said Hiram, proudly, "That's a true twenty-seven meter job. None of that coil-loaded stuff for me. I like a true *swr* reading."

"Huge," said Jeremy.

"Gigantic," agreed Alexis, "So, that's how you got the county authorities here ahead of us."

Hiram Cook's citizen band antennae resembled a giant box kite without paper. The rooftop monstrosity was among the last models sold before *good buddies* gave way to cell phones. It was motor driven to point in all directions, and slightly bent from wind damage. A black coaxial cable ran down the mast and into the upper room where Hiram kept his base station.

"Do you run heat, Hiram?" asked Alexis.

"I stay four watts and under," said Hiram Cook who had relayed his SOS to a neighbor with a thousand watt linear at home, and a 250 watt heater in his farm bus. Concluded Cook, "My neighbor alerted another *good buddy* who contacted the county sheriff's office. But, you get nobody's name unless I'm forced to take the oath."

"I'm not from the FCC," said Alexis.

"Now, can I ask you a question?"

"Of course, Hiram."

"How did state and federal officers get here so fast?" queried Cook, "When our tower's down we're stuck here in San Juan County. No cell phones, no land-lines, no computer text. We can't get a signal over those mountains, not even with CB skip."

"Chapman," explained Alexis in a word.

"My handyman, again?"

"Chapman's phone has satellite capabilities," said Alexis, "He could be anywhere on the globe and make contact. Anyway, he called me with an SOS."

"And you tracked him here?"

"No, he gave up this address," said the female general. Then, seeing the question mark on Cook's face, she added, "Somehow he has a text thread that leads to my phone."

"I don't text," said Hiram Cook.

"Lucky you," smiled Alexis.

"I have coffee inside," said Hiram, "You want a cup before you head out?"

"Thank you no," said Alexis Grumman, " I have a report to file."

QUANTUM ROOTS II

"Will you be sure to tell me," said Hiram Cook.

"Tell you what Sir.?"

"When you catch up to this fella."

"Sir, when we capture Olan Chapman," yelled back Alexis heading for the copter, "It will be front page news."

Chapter 36

T'was past midnight when Hiram strode through the sales outlet for Cookies Fine Wines. He pushed through an *off limits* doorway and stopped midway in a refrigerated unit that housed the wines. He hit a hidden button and a wall opened to reveal a secret room where Hiram kept his private selection of fine wines.

He peered into the darkness.

"You can come out, now." said Hiram.

Silence.

The secret room held expensive wines bought at exclusive wine auctions where Hiram was either lucky – or cagy enough - to be high bidder. Some bottles ran over a thousand dollars, and demanded perfect cooling temperatures around the clock.

"I hope you're not guzzling my good wine," said Hiram.

More silence. Then, body sounds emerged from the darkness.

"How did you know?' queried Olan Chapman emerging from the dirt dungeon.

"Half the world's looking for you," said Hiram,

QUANTUM ROOTS II

"When you didn't show up in the dragnet, I knew you were in here."

"Did we give 'em hell?" asked Olan dusting off shirt and trousers.

"We gave 'em bloody hell," said Hiram.

The two men walked outside and stopped by the burned out station wagon. Moonlight bounced off roof top areas where paint had melted away to bare metal.

"Sorry about the wagon," said Olan.

"I'm glad my car was in the house garage," said Hiram showing a slight smile.

"I needed the stick shift," said Olan.

"Of course," replied Hiram, "And I need to stop wasting money on wines and buy a second set of good wheels."

"Sounds like a decision," said Olan.

"It is," replied Hiram, "It's time Rebecca learns to drive."

"She would like that," said Olan, "And if you would like, I can set up Rebecca's laptop so it connects to the *hot spot* on her phone."

"That means going online?"

"That means going online," confirmed Olan.

"I suppose that step would come next," said Hiram Cook who feared losing Rebecca to the World

Wide Web, and it would be a giant step for Hiram who believed cyberspace was the dark side of the moon, or maybe even worse.

"Shadows are just shadows," replied the world renowned computer wizard, "And all is not just smoke and mirrors. I've been boning up on Dyspraxia in children, and while the body needs regulated exercise to curb motor slowness, the brain needs fresh fodder to form new alliances between mind and body."

Hiram Cook stared at Olan Chapman as though seeing the man for the first time. Suddenly the night air felt abnormally chilly, the distant mountains too dark to challenge. Said Hiram, "Why don't we go inside and share a bottle of wine."

Chapter 37

Come first light:

"Our farm bus will take you to the tunnel ," said Hiram as he and Olan stopped at driveway's end, "The pickers will get on. You will get off. When you exit the tunnel, you will be in Mexico."

"So, I get to see where the elusive pickers come from," smiled Olan.

"My neighbor Sudsy will be driving," explained Hiram, "We share the same pickers and split costs. He keeps the bus at his place."

"Sudsy is the guy who runs the heat?"

"A thousand watts," bragged Hiram.

"Before my time," said Olan.

"Shame," replied the owner of Cookies Fine Wines,, "You would have been a CB wizard."

The two men shook hands.

"One more favor?" asked Olan pulling a cell phone from an inner pocket.

"Name it."

"This is my last burner," said Olan, "It can't be

traced. The numbers in the back can't be traced. When the tower's back up, would you call my wife?"

"Done," said Hiram Cook, "Any message?"

"Make sure my rabbits are getting their Timothy Hay."

"Rabbits?" queried Hiram Cook.

"My rabbits," said the slender computer wizard, "It's important that my rabbits get their daily portion of Timothy Hay."

"His rabbits!" shrieked Ivy Chapman from Elks County N.J., two days later, "His freaking rabbits have taken over the park, our neighbor's park and closed down the interstate. You can't see the road for rabbits. You tell that little weasel to get his bony ass back here. The garbage disposal is busted, the toilet won't stop running. . . who the hell am I talking to anywhere ?"

"A friend," replied Hiram Cook trying to choke off a broadening smile, "Your husband is okay. He's safely in Mexico."

"Mexico?"

"Tijuana."

"He's into the tequila, isn't he?"

Meanwhile, back at DPA Headquarters in Virginia, Lt General, Alexis Grumman had a satellite visual switched to the big screen.

QUANTUM ROOTS II

"Is that who I think it is?" asked Jeremy Wade.

"It is," sighed Alexis popping a candy mint and taking a sip of ice water, "That's our boy, larger than life, carrying a whiskey bottle."

"Where is he?"

"On the San Mateo Bridge in California."

"California?" whistled Jeremy, "I thought he was in Mexico."

"We all thought he was south of the border."

"Can we nab him before he jumps?"

"Too late," replied Alexis, "He just jumped."

Epilogue

Rebecca Ann Cook went on to earn a BS degree in social services via an internet accredited college. She is currently married, has twin boys and works with autistic children in San Diego, California.

Federal agents rounded up The Black Hornets' international drug contacts, using data found in Carlton Lansbury's saddlebags.

Lt General, Alexis Grumman and Special Agent Jeremy Wade are back at the window booth in Nickles Bar & Grille, on one condition. Neither Alexis or Jeremy are to ever again, talk about anything that's small.

A random pleasure boat fished Olan Chapman from chilly bay side waters, and unwittingly let him go somewhere near the Golden Gate Bridge.

QUANTUM ROOTS II

KYLE KEYES

Public domain information taken from the Philadelphia Inquirer, Camden Courier Post, Bradenton Herald and Online Encyclopedia Wikipedia.

Topographic data supplied by Google Maps.

Point Shooting techniques come from a handbook written by Bobby "Lucky" McDaniel.

Cover pictures supplied by Free Digital art works and KDP Cover Creator

Footnote:
As of this writing, motor scooters can't fly, and worm holes only occur in apples.

www.ingramcontent.com/pod-product-compliance
Lightning Source LLC
Chambersburg PA
CBHW071259170626
46809CB00001B/285